Stone knew exactly what he had to do.

He'd known for weeks.

He had to pick up the pieces of his life—and Dahlia's, too—and he had to do it now. Tonight.

His life had broken apart one year ago, large pieces of it crushed beyond recognition. Even so, one piece, shining and pure, yet sharp enough to draw blood, a piece Stone could hold on to, was solid and it was real.

He was still deeply, hopelessly in love with Dahlia—and he'd do anything, absolutely *anything*—not to lose her.

Even if it meant he had to risk his heart all over again....

Dear Reader,

Silhouette Romance is proud to usher in the year with *two* exciting new promotions! LOVING THE BOSS is a six-book series, launching this month and ending in June, about office romances leading to happily-ever-afters. In the premiere title, *The Boss and the Beauty,* by award-winning author Donna Clayton, a prim personal assistant wows her jaded, workaholic boss when she has a Cinderella makeover....

You've asked for more family-centered stories, so we created FAMILY MATTERS, an ongoing promotion with a special flash. The launch title, *Family by the Bunch* from popular Special Edition author Amy Frazier, pairs a rancher in want of a family with a spirited social worker...and *five* adorable orphans.

Also available are more of the authors you love, and the miniseries you've come to cherish. Kia Cochrane's emotional Romance debut, *A Rugged Ranchin' Dad,* beautifully captures the essence of FABULOUS FATHERS. Star author Judy Christenberry unveils her sibling-connected miniseries LUCKY CHARM SISTERS with *Marry Me, Kate,* an unforgettable marriage-of-convenience tale. *Granted: A Family for Baby* is the latest of Carol Grace's BEST-KEPT WISHES miniseries. And COWBOYS TO THE RESCUE, the heartwarming Western saga by rising star Martha Shields, continues with *The Million-Dollar Cowboy.*

Enjoy this month's offerings, and look forward to more spectacular stories coming each month from Silhouette Romance!

Happy New Year!

Mary-Theresa Hussey

Mary-Theresa Hussey
Senior Editor, Silhouette Romance

Please address questions and book requests to:
Silhouette Reader Service
U.S.: 3010 Walden Ave., P.O. Box 1325, Buffalo, NY 14269
Canadian: P.O. Box 609, Fort Erie, Ont. L2A 5X3

A RUGGED
RANCHIN' DAD

Kia Cochrane

Silhouette

ROMANCE™
Published by Silhouette Books
America's Publisher of Contemporary Romance

For Keith

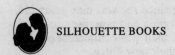 SILHOUETTE BOOKS

ISBN 0-373-19343-2

A RUGGED RANCHIN' DAD

Copyright © 1999 by Kia Jurkus

Printed in U.S.A.

Books by Kia Cochrane

Silhouette Romance

A Rugged Ranchin' Dad #1343

Silhouette Intimate Moments

Married by a Thread #600

KIA COCHRANE

reads anything she can get her hands on. "I love books with happy endings," Kia says, "especially romances." Kia, who has been writing since she was nine years old, was born and raised in Virginia and now lives in North Carolina with her husband, their white miniature poodle, their golden retriever and their new kitten.

Fabulous Fathers

Stone Tyler on Fatherhood...

I never thought much about faith—until mine was put to the test. You see, I blamed myself for my daughter's death last year. And I promised myself that nothing—absolutely nothing—would harm my little boy. Not if I could prevent it.

But I went about it all wrong. I took control of Field's life. I took away all the things that he cared about—just to keep him safe. But I forgot that kids need freedom as much as they need rules. And to be trusted nearly as much as they need to be loved.

I haven't been a good father to my son this past year. Haven't been much of a husband to Dahlia, either, to tell you the truth. But I'm trying to get past the grief and the guilt and to face the future with an open heart.

I just hope it's not too late....

Prologue

Dahlia walked toward the beckoning white light. She felt warm all over—and, finally, at peace. She hadn't felt this good since…well, since her hell on earth had begun twelve months ago.

The place was crowded. Everyone was lined up, waiting to get their wings, and to be escorted through the white gates. The guy in front of her wore brief bathing trunks, and he was carrying a surfboard, his shoulder-length blond hair still damp. He smelled faintly of salt and seaweed.

Dahlia sighed and glanced down at herself. She wasn't much better. She had on worn, faded jeans and a soft blue denim shirt. Odd, she had always believed entering heaven meant wearing white.

She glanced at the sentinel beside the gate. He wore a long, beautiful robe of ivory silk. He also had wings and a glorious halo to go along with his leather notebook and pencil. Maybe you weren't given white clothes until you passed through the gates.

Dahlia suppressed a sigh. What was taking so long? she

wondered. She was filled with anticipation and excitement. Your loved ones were supposed to be waiting for you, weren't they?

She bit her lower lip. Impatience was a trait she possessed in abundance, one that she wasn't proud of, and she tried hard to rein it in.

She did permit herself a small, bouncing motion on the balls of her booted feet, hoping to relieve some of her stress. She hated waiting in lines, but comforted herself with the knowledge that this line would be her last one ever.

Finally, *finally,* she reached the man with the wings and the halo.

"Your name, please?" he asked briskly.

"Dahlia Tyler."

"Ah, yes. Demise by being thrown from a horse."

"Actually, Firelight didn't throw me," she gently corrected him. "The branch of a tree knocked me to the ground."

"Ah, yes. Head injury," he said, as though that explained everything. "My name is Basil, and I am the Chief Angel. Here is a ticket for your wings and halo at the end of the path." He placed the ticket in her hand and immediately Dahlia found herself in a long white gown. Silk. Pure silk, she thought, running her hands over the material.

"Step through here, please."

Dahlia studied the gate he was holding open for her. She wanted to get out of this white mist, and go through the gate. It was clear on the other side.

She could see stone pathways through beautiful green fields, could hear the sound of rushing water somewhere beyond the gate, and she wanted very much to go there. She needed to go there, where it was safe and warm—but where was…?

"Mom! Over here!"

And Dahlia saw her. Brooke. Her daughter, standing on the path. She was wearing the long white gown, wings and halo of an angel. She looked so beautiful, Dahlia's heart ached. She hadn't seen her little girl in such a long time.

Twelve months, to be exact.

Her little girl. Her precious baby—no, not her baby. Brooke always hated it when she called her that. Brooke was gazing back at her with big blue eyes, her long dark hair loose and free, a wreath of white flowers on her head.

"Mom, hurry! I've been waiting and waiting for you!" Brooke held her arms out with a joyous smile.

Dahlia started to run toward her, but Basil stopped her with a gentle, but firm, hand. "There will be a short delay," he said quietly. "It has been brought to my attention—"

"Oh, no, please!" Dahlia cried. "Let me go through the gate now. I've waited so long for this," she pleaded with him. She *had* to make him understand! "I want to be with my daughter. I haven't held her or touched her in a year—"

"I am sorry, but there are rules, you know."

Basil did look as though he regretted keeping her out of heaven, but why couldn't he just let her go through the gate as planned? Why the delay? What had she done wrong?

"I've been standing in this line forever, waiting, waiting to be with my daughter." Dahlia was close to tears.

Basil's heavenly blue eyes rested gently upon her face. "It will only be three weeks," he promised her.

Dahlia looked wistfully at Brooke, who was still waiting on the path. Then she nodded slowly. After all, she wanted to make a good impression. She took a deep breath and almost saluted. "All right."

Basil looked pleased. "There is a man who is dangerously close to losing faith in himself. You are to help him find it."

Oh, great! "Who is this man?" she asked.

Basil checked his list, then looked at her for a moment that seemed to stretch endlessly between them. "His name is Stone Tyler."

Dahlia gasped. She'd never get into heaven now. There wasn't a snowball's chance in hell to get Stone to believe in anything. Not after what had happened to their daughter.

"This is top priority," he continued. "Stone Tyler is worth a little more effort."

"Yes, I know he is," Dahlia said softly. But she couldn't do it. She couldn't reach him. She'd tried and failed countless times before.

"Remember the power of love."

Dahlia sighed at the trust she saw in Basil's blue eyes. She peeked through the gate, but she could no longer see Brooke. Wearily she turned away.

Once again Basil stopped her with a gentle hand. "You have three weeks. If you do not complete your mission and return within the scheduled time, you may not go through the gate," he warned.

"I'll be here. I promise." Dahlia looked at the ticket in her hand. "Do I have to give this back?"

Basil shook his head. "No, it is yours to keep."

Dahlia stood still for a moment, frightened by the idea of leaving this place, and of the uphill battle ahead to restore Stone's faith in himself. But she would do it.

She had to.

She'd do whatever it took to be with her daughter again. Then she felt herself tumbling down, down, down....

Chapter One

Stone Tyler waited anxiously outside the hospital room while the doctor examined his wife. What in hell had he been thinking? Why had he spouted off about wanting to shoot Firelight? It wasn't the horse's fault that Brooke was dead.

He buried his face in his hands. If he hadn't said all those things about killing Brooke's golden palomino, then Dahlia wouldn't have—

Guilt piled on top of guilt, like so many layers of dirt and grime.

He wouldn't have shot Firelight. He wouldn't have taken his rifle out to the corral and put a bullet in his daughter's beloved horse.

He'd just been…frustrated. And angry.

At himself, mostly.

But why couldn't Dahlia understand that the ranch was no place for Field? He didn't want to lose his son, too. Why couldn't she understand how much he needed to keep his surviving son safe—no matter the cost?

Why couldn't she just let him do his job as a father?

Sending their ten-year-old boy to a boarding school in San Antonio was not the end of the world. Stone hated the idea of not seeing his son every day, but Field could come home on weekends. Dahlia acted as though San Antonio was on the other side of the country, instead of only sixty miles from the ranch.

He glanced up when he heard footsteps. It was the nurse. "You may see your wife now," she said. Her smile was reassuring.

He rushed to the door of Dahlia's room, the past couple of days crowding his mind. The argument, Dahlia racing off blindly to save Firelight, the way he'd found her, unconscious, in the meadow, the coma she'd been in for the past thirty-six hours...

Relief crashed in on him, flooding him with memories. It hadn't always been like this, Stone thought, as he hesitated outside the private room. Once there had been love and laughter.

Once he'd had a family. A *whole* family—with Dahlia, Field and Brooke.

Now it was breaking up all around him, and he didn't know how to stop it from happening.

Stone entered the room, the scent of roses and carnations assaulting him from all sides, reminding him of the flowers at Brooke's funeral.

And in the middle of the flowers, Dahlia lay still and silent in the white bed. But at least she was okay. The doctors had said so. All they'd been waiting for was Dahlia to wake up.

The doctor and nurse separated and let him pass between them, so he could bend over Dahlia's bed. Stone swallowed slowly, taking her limp hand in his. "Dahlia," he said quietly. "It's okay. Everything will be okay now. I promise."

He held his breath. He'd been talking to her for the past day and a half, hoping to get through to her. And then, a few minutes ago, she'd stirred and tried to open her eyes.

But what if she slipped back into a coma when she heard his voice this time? What if *he* was the reason she'd stayed unconscious for so long?

"Dahlia, open your eyes," Stone said tightly, his fingers gripping her hand like a lifeline. That was exactly what she was to him. His lifeline.

The center of his universe.

But she was going to leave him if he sent their son away.

"Dahlia." His voice was soft now, urging her to come back to him. "Dahlia, it's Stone. Open your eyes and look at me."

Her eyes opened and Stone looked into the violet-blue depths. The tip of her pink tongue slid out to lick her pale lips. "Stone," she said as she felt around her shoulder area with her free hand, frowning up at him in bewilderment.

"What is it, sweetheart? Does it hurt?" The pounding of his heart seemed to reverberate until the floor shook beneath his feet.

"Didn't I get my wings? Did they get crushed when I fell?"

There was a moment of hushed silence. Stone looked from his wife to the doctor.

"Your wife's had a severe blow to the head, Mr. Tyler," the doctor said quietly. "Give her some time."

Stone swallowed nervously, his gaze moving raggedly over Dahlia's face. Her head was bandaged, her blond hair spread out on the pillow. She was small anyway, but in the hospital bed she looked smaller and more helpless than he'd ever seen her.

"Stone." Her voice was only half a whisper. "What happened to my ticket?"

"Your ticket?" he asked.

"The ticket for my wings and halo. Basil gave it to me before he sent me back to earth." Her deep blue eyes, the color of the innermost part of a pansy, were fixed on him as she smiled. "He sent me back to help you," she said clearly, and then her eyes fluttered closed.

"Doc—" Stone felt full-scale panic wash over him.

"Mrs. Tyler's merely asleep." The doctor's voice was calm and reassuring.

But Stone felt anything but calm and reassured.

Apparently his wife believed she was an angel.

A week later, Stone signed all the necessary papers in order to take Dahlia out of the hospital and back to Lemon Falls and the ranch. According to the doctors, Dahlia was healthy enough to go home—even if she did still think she was an angel.

Stone turned as the nurse wheeled Dahlia out of her room. The woman smiled reassuringly at him. Different nurse, but the same smile of reassurance, he thought in exasperation.

"You ready?" he said to Dahlia, hoping she couldn't see how uneasy he felt. "I put your suitcase in the car."

She nodded, her blue gaze never leaving his.

He noticed how she sat quietly, without fidgeting. He wondered if Dahlia truly was strong enough to go home, or if her current demeanor was what the doctors meant by possible changes in her behavior.

As Stone guided his Ford Explorer through the heavy traffic in San Antonio, he kept stealing glances at his wife. Dahlia continued to sit quietly beside him, her hands folded primly in her lap. What was she thinking about? he wondered.

She'd always been so full of fire and energy and life, her

excitement at the promise of each new day contagious to all those around her, and a positive influence even at the blackest of times.

But Stone barely recognized the subdued woman sitting beside him now, the woman she'd become this past week.

For days now, he had avoided the subject of angels with Dahlia. And he'd constantly reassured the rest of the family that all she needed was some rest. But this morning he had his doubts.

"You okay?" he asked her, as they drove out of the city. "We can stop—"

"I just want to go home and be with my baby." Her voice was soft as it cut into his words. And his heart.

Stone's breath caught in his throat. Had she forgotten? Didn't she know that Brooke was—

"How is Field?" she asked slowly. "Really. How was he this morning?"

Stone was filled with sudden relief. She was talking about his son, not their daughter. Though Field was not Dahlia's biological child, she'd been his mother for most of his life.

Stone stole another glance at her. The heavy bandages had been removed from her head this morning, replaced by a much smaller one. Dahlia's hair, its shades of blond as varied as a Texas prairie, was pulled back in a ponytail, the soft bangs hiding most of the dressing.

But she looked so pale, he noticed with a sharp tug of guilt.

"He sounded okay when I talked to him on the phone," Dahlia continued. "But Field keeps things bottled up inside."

Like you.

That was one of the accusations she'd hurled at him before her accident, Stone remembered. And it was still between them, as solid and unrelenting as though the words had been carved in rock.

Dahlia turned in her seat and fixed him with her luminous, violet-blue gaze. "He told me you'd been reading and discussing *The Three Musketeers* with him before bed. That's wonderful."

"I always talk about books with him. What's so wonderful about it?" Stone was more curious than defensive. He took his eyes off the road long enough to glance at her.

"You haven't done that in a long time."

Their gazes mingled.

Stone abruptly tore his gaze away. He inhaled and exhaled quickly. He'd been halfway hoping that Dahlia's memory—the part that had to do with his so-called rejection of Field—wouldn't return.

"He needs you, Stone." Her voice was gentle. "He needs his father now more than ever."

"He's got me."

"But for how long?"

Stone shook his head slightly. He had no intention of rehashing old arguments. This was one discussion that'd had most of the tread worn off it already.

"Have you changed your mind about sending Field away?"

"We don't need to talk about this now." Stone tightened his grip on the steering wheel and kept his eyes on the road ahead.

Dahlia's hand stole over to touch his, and he felt the warmth, the softness, of her fingers. Slowly, carefully, some half-forgotten feelings stumbled to life. His heart started to race like a freight train, blood rushing through him, giving him life and energy and this fierce awareness of the woman sitting next to him.

He gently squeezed her hand and held it on the seat between them. If only…

"Have you changed your mind?" she repeated.

And the moment shattered like superfine crystal.

It left Stone with a broken, empty feeling inside, and a sense of having something so very close within his grasp sliding free. He wanted to give her the world. He'd lay down his own life for her. But he couldn't give Dahlia anything close to what she wanted from him.

"Damn it, Dahlia." His voice was low and rough with emotion. "You make it sound as though I'm sending him away as some sort of punishment. It's a good school," he insisted for perhaps the one millionth time.

"He loves it on the ranch." Still the same gentle voice.

Stone jerked his head around and met her steady gaze. "But Field is isolated from other kids his own age."

"Then you haven't changed your mind?"

He hesitated. He wanted to give her what she wanted. He wanted to make things right between them. But not at the expense of Field's safety. He couldn't take the chance.

"No," he said with deliberate gentleness. "I haven't changed my mind."

"Just you wait and see."

"What is that supposed to mean?" he demanded, his voice suddenly rough with exasperation—and with intense longing for the way things used to be between them.

Dahlia merely shrugged and smiled that calm, smug little smile of hers while entwining her fingers through his. Her touch was warm and possessive, and all thought literally flew out of Stone's mind.

All he knew was her touch.

Her velvety-soft fingertips. Her delicately shaped fingers. Her small hand with the square-cut diamond ring and matching white-gold wedding band.

He remembered the day he'd put those rings on her finger. The day he'd promised to love and cherish and protect her for all their days on earth. He'd meant every word of it, too.

Only…he hadn't been able to protect her.

Or their daughter.

Stone grew pensive and uneasy. How could Dahlia sit beside him so calmly after what had happened between them? His wife was not a calm person. She was warm, intense, playful, intelligent, willful, obstinate, impulsive, beautiful and impatient. But she was *not,* by any stretch of the imagination, calm!

Until this week. This week she was not only calm, but positively serene.

Like an angel.

Oh, Lord, he was losing it, Stone groaned from somewhere deep inside. The result of too little sleep, no doubt. And too much worry. But Dahlia had always looked like an angel—and now she was behaving like one!

"Dahlia, do you feel up to talking?" He asked the question gently because he didn't want to push her. But he had a lot on his mind, and some of it needed to be said as soon as possible.

"You want to talk to me?"

There was such bewildered surprise on her face and in her voice, that he cringed inside. He remembered the requests for conversation, for some kind of emotional connection these past twelve months. Requests that had slowly turned to angry demands and then to tearful begging.

Then they just…stopped.

"I think we should talk about what happened," Stone said slowly.

"About what happened?"

Stone kept his gaze fastened on the road ahead. "I

wouldn't have shot Firelight," he told her quietly. "I was angry and frustrated, and said a lot of stupid things I didn't mean. And I'm sorry. It's my fault you got hurt."

"I shouldn't have ridden off that way, without even waiting to saddle her first."

Stone felt her fingers curl up in his hand, the light scraping of fingernails against his flesh. He wanted so much to tell her how scared he'd been of losing her, how this week had been, to him, like stumbling clumsily out into the light after a year of sleepwalking through the darkness.

But he could wait and tell her that.

Right now he was enjoying the profound relief that she had forgiven him. The rest could come later.

He was especially enjoying the feel of her hand close and warm inside his. It had been a long time since she'd allowed him to touch her, to get this close, even for a moment or two. It had been months since they'd connected physically, in any way, shape or form.

That was mostly his fault, too.

Stone's mind skated back through the years. He'd been thinking a lot about their marriage this week. He'd taken a huge personal risk by letting himself fall in love with Dahlia nine years ago. Devastated by the way his ex-wife had abandoned him, with no warning, no explanation, just cold, calculated betrayal, he had been unable to see love and marriage in his future ever again.

Until he met Dahlia.

A warm, beautiful free spirit who'd been content to gloriously take each day as it came.

She'd been the healing balm to his wounded pride and broken heart. She'd taken him and his abandoned son and turned them into a family. Strong, loving and patient, Dahlia had guided him through a bad time in his life.

Now it was his turn. His turn to be strong. His turn to

guide them past the tragedy of Brooke's death to begin again. Only...how?

"Remember the first time I brought you to the ranch?" Stone tightened his grip on her hand.

A sweet, fleeting smile drifted over her face as she gazed up at him. "I was so scared, wondering if Blade and Rocky would like me."

"My brothers know a good thing when they see it." Stone grinned at her. "Wasn't it one of my brothers who played matchmaker and got us together in the first place?"

"Flint kept telling me about his big brother Stone—"

"For months he kept telling me about this new girl at college that he'd met and how he thought I'd like her—"

"And you kept stalling, not wanting to meet another female again for as long as you lived." Dahlia laughed.

Stone laughed, too. They'd done this countless times before, each giving their version of his brother Flint's one and only attempt at matchmaking.

"I was still scared when it came time to meet the rest of your family, though." Dahlia shifted slightly in her seat and leaned her head back. "I took classes with Flint, but meeting your other two brothers—and especially your baby boy—was a big day in my life."

"And meeting you was a big day in mine," Stone told her softly, taking his eyes off the road long enough to look at her. Dahlia's eyes were a startling, dazzling shade of blue, a dark, velvety contrast to her pale gold skin and sunny blond hair. "The most important day in my life."

He watched for a second or two as her blue eyes darkened and deepened in wonder, and shock waves of longing splintered through him.

"Was it, Stone?"

The wistful note in her voice wrenched at something hidden far back in the boarded-up places of his heart. How long had it been, he wondered uneasily, since he'd said anything even remotely reassuring to her?

"You know it was," he answered, suddenly feeling too much, needing too much from her.

Taking several deep, steady breaths, he concentrated on the traffic, unable to trust his tenuous self-control. They were on a two-lane, paved country road now, and the light, morning traffic was a welcome distraction.

So were her fingers, snuggled deep inside his hand. Her closeness eased the ache of emptiness that had tormented him the past year. It had been so long since she'd wanted anything to do with him, either physically or emotionally.

Grief over Brooke's death had taken its toll.

Stone grew still as he remembered the one exception. Nine months ago, Dahlia had decided she wanted another baby—but he'd had to refuse.

Something else she'd wanted that he couldn't, in good conscience, give to her. Because there was no way in hell that he'd bring another child into this world, to love it, care for it...

And then lose it.

The melting ice around Stone's heart slowly hardened.

Dahlia watched as Stone drove the rest of the way to the ranch, both hands now gripping the steering wheel. Watched the way he'd withdrawn, once again, into that lonely, private place deep inside himself.

Brooke's death had absolutely destroyed him, she acknowledged, as fear and doubt swept through her. He wasn't going to let her help him. And here she was, with only two weeks left to complete her mission!

Two weeks—when she'd been trying to get through to him for twelve long, painful months.

But Stone's will, as always, was one of pure steel.

How could she possibly make him believe in anything ever again? How could she make him see what a terrific father he was? And that what he needed to do now, most of all, was to trust his feelings when dealing with Field. How could she hope to restore his faith in himself, to trust his own good judgment again?

But that was her mission from Basil.

Oh, dear, how was she to accomplish this particular miracle all by herself?

Dahlia knew how hard it was to let Field be a normal little boy, to protect him without controlling his every move, to love him without smothering him—but Stone wasn't even trying.

He was so wrapped up in grief and guilt over Brooke's death, and fear over losing Field, that he wasn't listening to anyone.

She straightened her shoulders. She wanted so much to be a good angel, to live up to the trust that Basil had placed in her. But Stone—he wasn't the same man she'd married. He'd always wanted more, craved more, fought for more than anyone she'd ever met. But the fight had gone out of him.

And so had all the love.

Dahlia could still feel the warmth of his fingers around hers, even though he was no longer holding her hand. But his touch lingered in her mind far longer than she cared to admit.

Memories tapped at her heart.

The gentleness that had an unexpected way of peeking through Stone's oh-so-tough outdoorsy personality. The startling chemistry that had sprung to life upon meeting face-to-face the first time. And the way the sexual attraction had grown and deepened through the years.

Stone was more than her husband. He was her best friend.

Which made his...his almost studied emotional distance doubly hard to take. Stone had preferred to live in an emotional vacuum since Brooke's death, to become isolated from pain—but he was forcing the rest of them to live that way, as well.

Dahlia's gaze repeatedly strayed toward Stone's side of the car. It was hard to believe that the man who had once made her nerve endings sing with joy could cause her heart to ache so much. But when Brooke died, he'd closed off the part of his life that had to do with being happy. He'd also, by all appearances, closed and locked the part of his heart that had to do with love. And he had no desire to open either one.

Her sigh was soft, and with an effort she pulled herself out of her thoughts. She had work to do, and she was going to do it. But where was she to start?

"I remember the morning we brought Brooke home from the hospital," she said brightly. She desperately wanted to gain back some of the closeness that had vanished when Stone had retreated behind one of his moods. "She was wearing that little denim dress embroidered with little red hearts on the collar..."

"And you tied a red ribbon around her little bald head."

Dahlia was surprised at the way he joined in. She wasn't used to talking about Brooke and having him respond. Usually he tried to change the subject.

"She wasn't bald," Dahlia protested, laughing. "She had hair in the back almost long enough to put into a ponytail."

Stone hesitated and then his words came out sort of gruff and tender. "She was the prettiest little thing I'd ever seen in my life."

Tears backed up in her throat. Especially when Stone reached out and took her hand in his again. "Was she as pretty as Field?"

"Guys aren't pretty." But he sent her a fleeting grin. "Field was a rugged little guy even on his first day of life." Then his grin broadened. "All six pounds of him."

Dahlia saw the light in his gray eyes just seconds before he turned his attention back to the road ahead. But he squeezed her hand in his, and she squeezed back. And then she had a thought.

"Why don't you have any pictures of Field during his first year?"

"What do you mean?" Stone sped up to pass a car.

"You only have four or five pictures of him—"

"We've got dozens of albums, crammed full of pictures of both kids." Stone was back in his own lane now and flashed her a puzzled, questioning look.

"But all those were taken after we met. After we were married," Dahlia explained. "I meant pictures of Field coming home from the hospital. Do you realize there are no pictures of your son with his mother?"

He looked at her. "You're his mother."

She smiled gently at him, touched by the statement. For Stone, his first wife and the mother of his child just…no longer existed. Not in his mind. And certainly not in his heart. "But why didn't you take more?" she asked him. "Field was your firstborn son. I would have thought you'd have taken tons of pictures."

Stone shrugged and turned his attention back to the road. But he didn't evade the question. "I don't have a reason. I guess I was just too busy taking care of him to bother with taking pictures."

And too hurt.

Dahlia suddenly cringed inside at the thought of what

her completing her mission would mean for Stone. He'd already been abandoned by one woman, and he'd never understood her reason.

And now, if things worked out, Dahlia would also abandon him. Would he understand? Would he understand she just had to be with Brooke? No matter what the cost?

And Field…oh, that poor, poor child. Dahlia's heart wrenched with guilt at just the thought of leaving him. He'd already been abandoned by one mother. What would her leaving do to his ability to trust?

That was why she had to get Stone and Field's relationship on solid ground. Before it was time for her to leave.

"I'm sorry now that I didn't take more pictures of Field his first year," Stone was saying, and she struggled to pay attention. "Kids grow up so fast and then they're…gone," he ended quietly.

Dahlia watched as he struggled with some painful memory. She said gently, "Field's growing every day. It's hard to believe he's already ten years old."

"Yeah."

"Soon he'll be in high school and dating some cute little cheerleader."

Stone cleared his throat. "More than likely some little cowgirl in a rodeo."

"All he talks about is entering rodeo roughstock events when he's old enough." Dahlia saw the life drain from his eyes and added softly, "He wants so very much to be like you when he grows up."

"I know." Profound weariness settled over his lean features.

"It's natural for a son to want to be like his dad," she continued.

"Then I wish I'd been a lawyer or something like that," Stone snapped, his pain and frustration close to the surface.

Dahlia drew in a fast, agonized breath and said nothing. What was the use? Everything she said to him came out wrong. Everything she did only made him feel worse.

"Dahlia...honey, I'm sorry." He turned to her and tried to smile. "I didn't mean to take your head off. I just wish I hadn't told Field all those wild and wonderful stories about my rodeo days. It put ideas in his head."

She laughed soft and low. "It'll be years before he's old enough to compete. Field's exploring his options, that's all. He'll go through weeks of wanting to be a rodeo champion and then a concert pianist or a great painter—"

Stone hooted with laughter. "A concert pianist? Field? A rock musician, maybe, but give me a break. Field's about as likely to play classical music as I am to sprout wings and fly."

Dahlia grinned happily. Somehow she'd gotten him to laugh and that was a good feeling. And a good start.

She glanced out the window at the passing countryside, with its bluestem and buffalo grass. They were in the hill country now, driving along the Medina River, so they were almost at the ranch.

Stone turned onto a dirt road, lined with mountain cedar trees, and she breathed in the characteristic fragrance of the hill country. Stone took the bridge across the river and moments later they drove under the large sign, proclaiming: Tyler Ranch. Established 1900.

Field was the fourth generation of Tylers to live on the 750-acre spread. Dahlia knew it would break his heart not to grow up here like his father and uncles.

And it would break Stone's heart, too, even if he was too stubborn to admit it.

She propped her elbow in the open window, her chin in her hand, and gazed out at the miles of whitewashed fencing crisscrossing the range. She stared longingly out at the herds of sheep grazing in the foothills, the young lambs frolicking after their mothers. She sighed heavily.

A big, white three-story Victorian house, nestled in a grove of very old oak and pecan trees, came into view. An enormous red barn stood behind it, off to one side. As always, she felt a flash of pride when she saw the place where she had come to live as a bride of twenty-one.

That had been nine years ago, she thought, as Stone parked in the circular driveway.

A lifetime ago.

The car door on her side was yanked open. Stone's youngest brother, Rocky, escorted her gently across the driveway and up the porch steps. "We're glad you're home," he said with a grin. "Gives us an excuse to throw you a welcome-home barbecue tonight."

Dahlia smiled up at him, wondering where Field was hiding. "You Texas boys certainly do love to eat, don't you?" she teased back.

"How did you ever guess that?" Rocky's grin widened as he settled her on the porch swing. Rocky had a huge appetite for barbecued ribs and hot Texas chili, but he was cowboy-lean, and had women chasing him from three counties. "Field made you a pitcher of lemonade, all by himself," her brother-in-law said, his voice low for her ears alone. "So pretend you like it."

Rocky never changed, Dahlia thought gratefully, her gaze following Stone as he came up the front steps, carrying her suitcase. Just then the screen door flew open and Dahlia's ten-year-old stepson rushed out onto the porch, carrying a glass of lemonade. He headed straight for the porch swing and thrust it toward Dahlia. "I made it myself. All by myself," he added with a sidelong look at his father.

Dahlia took a sip, announced it was perfect and drank up as the little boy she'd raised almost from birth watched with anticipation. He was slender and dark like his dad, with Stone's gunmetal gray eyes.

"Don't I get a hug?" she asked the child she loved with all that was left of her heart.

Field hesitated. "Uncle Rocky said to be careful and let you hug me."

Dahlia smiled and reached out with one hand to draw the little boy closer. "Thank you for being so thoughtful, sweetie," she said, kissing his cheek. "And thank you for the lemonade. It's delicious."

Rocky returned to the porch, carrying a tray with the pitcher of lemonade and three glasses. There were also three different kinds of cookies. "Field went with me to the store this morning," Rocky said with a wink.

"Don't you like your lemonade, Dad?" Field asked, staring up at his father. Stone leaned against the porch railing, absently rubbing his fingertip along the rim of the glass he held. "I made it," the little boy announced, a slight trace of defiance in his voice. "All by myself."

"It's good," Stone said after taking a hasty sip. "Excellent."

"I cut the lemons in half with a knife." Field was eyeing Stone carefully. "And, boy, was it sharp!"

Dahlia's breath caught in her throat. She saw Stone dart a swift glance in his brother's direction.

"I was in there watching him," Rocky said hurriedly, shifting uneasily on the porch railing where he was perched.

"But even if he wasn't," Field chimed in, "I could've done it. Because I'm not a baby." That last statement came out as if he dared someone, anyone—especially Stone—to disagree with him.

Stone must have realized it, too, because he stated quietly, "No, you're not a baby. And knives aren't dangerous as long as you know how to use them."

"I know how. Uncle Rocky taught me," Field added helpfully, his gray eyes brightening.

Nearby, Dahlia heard Rocky's low, rueful groan. Her gaze darted to her husband. Stone had practically raised his youngest brother, and now he fixed him with a long, level look of reproach.

"Uncle Rocky said you gave him a knife when he was my age," Field piped up, making matters worse.

Dahlia saw the startled look in Stone's gray eyes. He slowly set his glass of lemonade down on the porch railing. "Did Uncle Rocky give you a knife?" he asked gently.

Field hesitated, then darted a sudden sheepish look at Rocky. The little boy looked back at his father and slowly nodded. Pulling a small leather pouch out of the back pocket of his jeans, Field said, "He gave me the one that you gave to him."

Instead of taking the knife away from his son, Stone merely asked, "And Rocky taught you how to use it?"

Field nodded. "This morning while we waited for the lemonade to get done."

"After you finish drinking your lemonade, why don't you ask your uncle Rocky to give you some more lessons?" Stone surprised everyone by saying.

Dahlia's heart surged with hope as she saw the look of pure joy enter Field's eyes.

Field and Rocky finished their cookies and lemonade in record time, and headed toward the barn. If she turned around, Dahlia would be able to see them. And she could certainly hear them as Rocky patiently taught the little boy how to handle the pearl-handled knife. She smiled at the laughter that drifted up to the porch.

"That was a wonderful thing you did, letting Field keep the knife," Dahlia said, smiling cheerfully.

Stone shrugged. "A boy needs to learn how to handle himself. That includes weapons."

"It means more than learning how to handle himself, Stone," she said earnestly. "Letting him have the knife means you trust him."

Stone drained the last of his lemonade and set the glass down on the tray. "It means I think he's old enough to go away to school." His voice was carefully low and even. "He's right. He isn't a baby. And he'll do just fine at boarding school."

"But, Stone—"

His gray eyes leveled on her. "He leaves two weeks from today." Then he scooped up her suitcase and headed for the screen door. "I'll put this in your room."

Stone entered the house and shut the screen door behind him. It was more gentle than a slam, but much harder than merely closing the door, Dahlia noticed wryly.

Two weeks. In two weeks Field would be sent away.

Dahlia turned around in the swing, fixing her gaze on Field, out by the barn. Basil said if she didn't return within three weeks, then she couldn't return. One week had already passed. In the hospital.

So she had two weeks left.

She took a deep breath and let it out in a rush. If she could only stop Stone from sending Field to that boarding school in San Antonio, if she could convince him that living on the ranch would not put Field in danger—then maybe he'd regain his faith that he could protect his son.

She sighed, watching Stone's little boy practice throwing his knife at the barn door, over and over and over again, determined to make his mark on the paper target. And

Dahlia knew that keeping Field on the ranch wouldn't alone solve the problem.

It was a start, but she now clearly understood the mission Basil had entrusted to her. She had to restore Stone's faith in himself, and in his ability to take care of his family— even if it meant letting go herself.

Chapter Two

The Tyler family and the ranch hands mingled freely at the barbecue later that night. Three picnic tables had been placed end to end on the brick terrace, laden with bowls of barbecued chicken, potato salad, baked beans and barbecued ribs. A separate picnic table held the desserts.

Stone stood to one side, a bottle of beer in his hand that he didn't really want, and watched the camaraderie of the others. Music played softly in the background, a mix of jazz and classical. Rocky had confiscated some of Dahlia's favorite CDs from her collection.

Stone had a sudden, intense memory of dancing in the rose garden with Dahlia on summer nights. Dancing in the moonlight, with only the stars for company and a CD player for the soft music she loved.

And when she'd touched him, the world had spun and split and lightning had flashed.

He sighed heavily, his thoughts stumbling reluctantly back to the present. Stone knew Dahlia couldn't help what she felt—or what she believed. One of the doctors thought it could be a combination of her head injury and the trauma of Brooke's death. That believing she was an angel was Dahlia's own way of dealing with her grief.

And it was about time she did deal with it, Stone knew. For the past year, Dahlia had been in a major state of denial, behaving as though nothing had changed. When everything had.

Brooke was gone and there was nothing any of them could do about it.

Stone continued to stand there on the terrace, the relentless music stirring his blood and making him think about days, and nights, that weren't all that long ago. And he had the urgent need to escape from all this family fun and togetherness.

Before he forgot this wasn't real life.

Real life was hard work.

And if Stone hung around having fun and feeling relaxed and mellow, he would want more—and he'd want it to last.

And that wasn't going to happen.

Because what was life without Brooke in it? What did it mean to live a normal life without his daughter here, too?

Stone's thoughts strayed back to that August summer night, a year ago. They'd had a barbecue that evening, too. A big one, to celebrate Stone and Dahlia finally building a house of their own.

To celebrate…life.

It had felt so damned good to be alive that night, he remembered painfully. He had felt incredibly lucky. And incredibly blessed.

Blessed with good health and work he enjoyed. With men who were more than ranch hands, they were his friends. And with three brothers he wouldn't trade a ton of gold for, no matter how irritating and meddlesome they could be.

But most of all he'd felt blessed to have Dahlia in his life—and to have fathered the two children he loved more than anything on this earth.

Field had been the only good thing that had come out of his disastrous first marriage. And Brooke had been the icing on the cake when he'd thought life couldn't get any better after he'd married Dahlia.

He remembered that night a year ago this month, and how he'd been looking forward to having at least one more child. But that was back when he'd believed his kids would live to grow up.

When he'd believed he could keep his children safe and whole to grow up to live a full life.

Stone took a slow, deliberate swallow of the cold beer.

That next morning, Brooke had taken her horse out alone, without permission, the high-spirited, beautiful little mare he'd given her on her birthday just six weeks earlier. Firelight had been spooked by something—and had thrown Brooke headfirst into the river.

So okay, damn it, maybe he hadn't been the most spontaneous and open-hearted of fathers this past year. That was still no reason for Dahlia to have accused him of neglecting his own child.

He didn't want his little boy hurt. Did that make him hard? Or controlling?

Not in his mind, it didn't.

He was a father trying to protect his son the best way he knew how.

Stone took another deep swallow of his beer. He didn't have it in him to act as though nothing had happened to his little girl. He couldn't go on living as though Brooke hadn't died. He couldn't pretend everything was just like before, that life could, and should, go on without her.

Because it couldn't.

Because to go on without her was to leave Brooke behind.

"Hey—" his older brother, Blade, slapped a hand on his shoulder "—why so anti-social tonight?"

Stone glanced at him. And he felt raw suddenly, twelve months' worth of healing ripped away to expose the fragility of what lay within. It was always like this as soon as he started to remember. As if Brooke had been killed only yesterday.

"You okay?" Concern was plainly written on Blade's thin, angular face.

Stone shrugged, his gaze wandering across the terrace until he located Dahlia. She was wearing a stone-washed denim dress and red sandals, and she looked fantastic. Her blond hair was hanging loose, just brushing her shoulders, the moonlight and lantern light playing with the different shades of gold and wheat and tan.

A sharp blast of old-fashioned desire heated his thoughts. She was gently beautiful, and that beauty captivated him.

"You'd never know she just got out of the hospital this morning," Blade quietly remarked, following his gaze.

Stone nodded absently, hearing the music of Vivaldi pulsate through the summer night—and him. Stirring memories of making love with Dahlia and holding on and being there for each other, no matter what.

Stirring memories of all the things they'd lost.

They had separate bedrooms now, and they'd had them for quite some time. Because Stone hadn't known how to go about getting his wife back into their room. He flashed on waking up with her in a tumble of pastel cotton sheets, her silky blond hair and sleep-warm flesh resting gently against his body. Snuggling and talking with her early in the morning, before the ranch was awake and the workday kicked into high gear, had been some of the best times in their marriage.

Because he could always talk to Dahlia. There was nothing he couldn't say to her without knowing she'd understand.

Until Brooke was killed.

Then, to talk about it made it seem too real to him.

Blade spoke quietly beside him. "Brooke...was like Dahlia in a lot of ways. Impulsive."

Stone was startled at the way his older brother stumbled over Brooke's name, as though Blade didn't know whether or not to say his niece's name out loud. Is this what grief did to people? Stone wondered. Robbed them of the freedom to speak their minds? Or had he done this to his family by dismissing them whenever they dared to speak his daughter's name?

But Stone already knew the answer.

Stone and his three brothers had been raised by their father after their mother died. The one thing they all had in common was saying what was on their minds. No matter what.

So Stone found this careful, almost gentle treatment from his older brother to be nearly too much for him to handle.

Impulsive? Stone thought bitterly. Is that what his daughter had been? To get on a horse alone, without permission—something she'd been told a dozen times not to do?

Did that make him any less responsible for her death?

He'd given her the horse.

Blade continued as though Stone was taking part in the conversation. "Dahlia's also sensitive and emotional," he said slowly. "And I have to admit I didn't think she'd make it as a rancher's wife. But she's a tough one when the chips are down. That is one determined lady when she thinks she's right."

"What are you getting at?" Stone didn't have a clue. His three brothers had been keeping their collective mouths shut lately, for some unfathomable reason.

Blade's voice became very quiet. "I think Dahlia's right about Field staying here on the ranch."

Ah, Stone was beginning to see the light. He looked curiously at the man who had been left in charge of the family—and the ranch—when their father had died when Stone was twenty.

"Raising a child alone is not easy," Blade said. "And you know that better than anyone."

Stone grew still. He'd never forget the shock of his first wife running off in the middle of the night shortly after Field was born. The endless diapers and round-the-clock feeding schedule had kept him hopping those first few months of his son's life.

Hastily shaking off the memory, he said, "But I'm not raising—"

"Dahlia said she was leaving if you sent Field away to school, didn't she?" Blade was obviously losing patience with him. "You might just find yourself living without her if you don't watch your step."

Stone was surprised into silence. There was little privacy on the ranch, with Blade and Rocky both living in the same house with them. And Stone didn't like the fact that what went on between him and his wife was being constantly observed by the rest of his family.

Especially since Brooke had died.

"Field is the firstborn male heir to the Tyler ranch," Blade stated flatly. "You're taking his birthright away from him." Then he walked away without another word.

Stone watched him join Rocky and several of the ranch hands, and he suppressed the urge to strangle his brother.

Blade, of all people, should understand that he only wanted the best for his son.

He tipped the bottle of beer to his mouth and took another long swallow. It looked as though this day was never going to end.

Dahlia watched Blade walk away from Stone, and she wondered what they had been talking about so intently. Blade was not an easy man to know, but from the beginning he'd always been kind to her and made an effort to make her feel part of the family.

Had they been arguing? About what?

Oh no, over *her?* Usually when Stone and Blade disagreed, they did so in private. Never within earshot of the men who worked for them. And never at a party.

The two men were close in age, and it was natural for them to be at odds on a regular basis. Stone had dropped out of college after two years because their father had died, and he believed Blade had needed him at home.

Stone handled the business end of the ranch, all the accounting, which included taxes, contracts, loans and payroll, leaving Blade free to run the ranch. But, even though Blade had been appointed Flint and Rocky's legal guardian after their dad was killed, Stone had always been actively involved in every decision concerning his two younger brothers as well as the ranch.

So conflict had always been part of Stone's relationship with Blade.

But Dahlia didn't want them arguing over her.

She stole another look at the man who was her husband, and took a deep, hard breath. Stone hadn't changed much over the years. His straight, dark hair still brushed the collar of his denim shirt. He still had the same lean face and prominent cheekbones, his gray eyes wary and watchful when he was troubled.

It had been love at first sight—for both of them—and they'd been married three months later. Dahlia had loved being a sheep rancher's wife, and mother to his fifteen-month-old son. And thirteen months later Brooke had been born, making their lives complete.

Dahlia was quietly happy as she remembered the birth of her first child. If Stone had felt trapped by the idea of becoming a father again, he had certainly never shown it.

He had absolutely adored Brooke from the moment he'd first laid eyes on her. And Dahlia would never forget the joy she'd felt holding Stone's child in her arms.

Her child.

She felt a hand on her shoulder and looked up to find Stone standing next to her chair. "Flint and Shannon are here. Suppose we go and greet them."

"Of course."

An assistant professor of English lit at UT in San Antonio, Flint was the only brother who didn't make his living from ranching. But you'd never know it to look at him, Dahlia thought with a smile as she rushed to hug him. He had the same lean, dark, good looks as his brothers. Dressed in boots and jeans, he could easily pass as a cowboy.

"You didn't wait dinner on the two of us, did you?" Flint asked, holding her away from him to take a good look. But he seemed satisfied that she was okay.

"We certainly did." Dahlia smiled back at him, then knelt to say hello to his little girl. "Shannon, how are you?" she asked the tiny six-year-old, with the dark brown ponytail and huge gray-green eyes.

Dahlia felt the pain, swift and sharp, as she gazed upon the little girl who looked so much like Brooke. The same dark hair, heart-shaped face and sweet, crooked little smile.

"I'm fine. How are you?" Shannon asked her shyly.

Dahlia hid a grin. "Did your daddy tell you not to hug me?" When Shannon nodded, she said, "I sure could use a hug."

Shannon tumbled into her arms almost before the words left Dahlia's mouth, holding Dahlia tightly around the neck, a short little sob escaping from somewhere deep inside the little girl.

"It's okay, sweetie," Dahlia whispered, loving the solid feel of her. And she felt a sense of shame, deep within, for neglecting one of her most favorite people in the world.

She hadn't spent much time with Shannon since Brooke had died. Tightly wrapped up in her own pain and grief, she hadn't been able to be around the child who reminded her so much of all that she'd lost.

How was Shannon handling life without Brooke to share everything with? Dahlia wondered uncertainly. The two little girls had been very close. More like sisters than cousins.

More to the point—how was Shannon handling Dahlia's apparent rejection of her all these months? Flint's wife had died when Shannon was a baby, and Dahlia was the closest thing to a mother the child had ever known.

This was another situation she had to correct as quickly as possible. She'd been told that Flint and Shannon were spending the weekend at the ranch, so she hugged the little girl again and suggested, "What do you say to a picnic tomorrow—just you, me and Field?"

"Really?" The child's gray-green eyes were shining with happiness. "A real and true picnic with you and Field? Just like we used to?"

Dahlia swallowed slowly and nodded. She managed a smile, but tears filled her eyes as she felt the tug of love coming from her little niece. But she had to stay focused on her mission to restore Stone's faith—so she could get into heaven.

It was the only way she could ever be with Brooke again.

Even so, she couldn't help but revel in the fact that she had been the only woman on the ranch for years. Even the cook was a man. And up until a year ago, she'd loved playing mom to her extended family, as well as to her own child.

But without Brooke…

Dahlia felt wrenched in two. She'd forgotten how much she loved everyone here tonight—and how much they loved her.

Except for Stone.

Dahlia couldn't look up without finding his gaze pinned on her tonight. Sometimes she didn't even need to look up. She'd always been able to sense his presence. Now, she caught Stone watching her with that cool, expressionless gaze that masked his emotions, and her stomach tightened in anguish.

It tightened even more when he spoke to her.

"Would you like to take a walk in the rose garden?" Stone's voice was low and for her ears alone. "I know how much you like to look at the roses in the moonlight."

Surprise couldn't begin to explain the way she felt inside. How long had it been since he'd asked her to go for a walk with him? And alone in the moonlight?

Not for a year, at least.

Dahlia nodded and they moved around the crowd of family and friends, until they reached the path that led to her garden. The first year she married Stone, Dahlia had planted ten yellow rosebushes. And each year after that she'd planted ten more, until now she had ninety rosebushes of all colors, bordered by neatly trimmed hedgerows—a living testament to the way their marriage had thrived and bloomed over the years.

She stared in silence at the ten rosebushes she'd planted this past spring. The magnificent yellow roses, with their delicate pink shadings at the edge of the petals, reminded her of Brooke.

Stone led her to the bench and she sat down to gaze up at the stars. Music filled the air, and she had a sudden, vivid memory of dancing out here on summer nights. She could almost feel Stone's arms around her, close and warm, the scent of roses drifting through the air.

The night sky dark and soft.

The million stars slowly appearing one by one.

And the two of them so much in love it hurt even to think of being separated for a night.

They would dance for hours, alone in their own, private little world. A world built on love and trust and sharing more than a bed. They'd shared their lives with each other, both the good and the bad.

Until last year.

Dahlia watched Stone as he seated himself next to her and wondered what he was thinking by dragging her away from the party this way. She didn't mind, it was something he used to do all the time—but why now? And why to-night?

Her gaze raked curiously over his face, and she found herself thinking his eyes were the soft gray of a well-worn dime as longing ravaged his face.

"The roses are beautiful," she told him nervously. "Who's been taking care of them while I was in the hos-pital?"

"I have."

Another surprise. Dahlia smiled tentatively at him, and he shrugged. But she noticed a grin was forming.

"I weeded and watered them, sprayed for bugs and dead-headed the blooms that had faded," he explained.

Dahlia's smile widened. "You did a great job," she told him softly. She was so touched by his effort to care for something she loved so much, she could barely speak.

Lately, Stone hadn't paid much attention to the things she held dear to her heart. And yet, he'd taken care of her rose garden. Why the sudden change? she wondered. And why, oh why, couldn't he make the same effort with Field?

Stone seemed to hesitate, and then he slid his hand into hers. "I wanted you to come home and find the rose garden had been tended to in your absence."

"Thank you." She listened for a moment, listened to the muted laughter of the others, the music in the distance. She tried not to flinch at those long, searching looks of his, which slid along her nerve endings like stroking fingers. But it was so very hard to respond to them, to open her heart to him again.

He'd closed himself off from her after Brooke's death. Slammed the lid down hard on everything good in their lives. Consumed with guilt, he had trashed their plans for their new house and another baby, and then decided to send his sweet, precious son away from her.

It was as though her wishes were no longer important—or real—to him. As though she no longer mattered.

And sometimes...sometimes when she was able to come out of her own pain and grief, she had to wonder if he even still loved her.

"Let's dance," Stone suggested. He got to his feet, leaving Dahlia to gaze blankly up at him.

He wanted to dance? With her? Out here in the moonlight as they used to do?

Stone pulled her gently to her feet and into his arms. His hands slid easily around her waist, leaving her no choice but to place hers on his shoulders. She tensed as he drew her closer, the months of being alone, of sleeping alone, making the physical contact with him awkward, yet sweetly erotic.

It was as though they were strangers, and Dahlia hadn't felt this aware of him, in quite this way, since the very early days of their relationship. When she was first beginning to know him. When Stone was still raw and hurting from his ex-wife's desertion and trying desperately not to fall in love again.

When, as an only child of an Air Force pilot, Dahlia hadn't had much experience with concepts like roots or security or permanence. She'd lived in eighteen places her first twelve years of life. By the time she was in second grade, she'd learned not to make friends because it hurt too much to say goodbye.

It felt almost like the first time Stone had held her, she kept thinking as they moved slowly to the music. When he'd been scared of losing his heart all over again, and she'd never allowed herself to get close enough to put hers at risk. When the sexual attraction, bursting to life between them, had mingled with their mutual fear and distrust.

Dahlia couldn't suppress the tremor that slid through her, and Stone asked, "Are you cold?"

She shook her head. She was far from feeling cold. Stone's hands had always had the tendency to stray and tonight was no different. And neither was the path of fire his hands left wherever they touched.

Stroking her back.

Kneading gently under her shoulder blades.

Drifting slightly below her waist to rub the small of her back.

Dahlia took a deep, slow breath and buried her face in his shoulder, breathing in the smell of freshly washed denim and warm male flesh. The classical music stopped for an instant, and then the haunting sound of jazz pulsated toward them, the horns slow and seductive and stirring.

Without thinking, just feeling, she moved against him to the beat of the music. Her arms slid down to hang limply at her sides, while she moved the lower half of her body into the lean, hardening strength of him.

And then she gazed up into deepening, darkening gray eyes.

Stone's arms tightened convulsively around her waist, bringing her up hard and close to him. Dahlia moved back only slightly, still holding his gaze, moving with the soul-stirring beat, away from him—and into him. Keeping time to the music and losing herself in the seductive rhythm of the horn solo on the CD.

It had been so long…too long…since she'd felt this good. This alive. This…happy.

And she let the memories and the look and feel of Stone fill her mind and heart. The familiar scent and feel of him overwhelmed her with a wild sense of being thrown back in time.

Before the distance between them had grown into an impasse.

Before the pain…and the guilt.

Before their lives had been blown all to hell on that terrible August morning a year ago.

She could see the same need in Stone's eyes that was stumbling to life in her. The strength of that need, that raw lightning bolt of desire, was a live thing, flashing, twisting, spinning between them and drawing both of them closer to the edge.

A fresh trembling, terrifying need raced through her.

Hot…

Hungry.

Her movements slowed. Held against the hot steel of Stone's body, she stared up at him as one song ended and another began. This, too, was slow. Romantic. And time, instead of thrusting her backward through the years to a better, stronger relationship with him, had now stopped completely.

Leaving them frozen.

Somewhere alone. Without fear. Without history—or a future.

All that mattered was this one shining moment, this tiny slice of time that had everything to do with what was happening now, at this very second. And when Stone kissed her, she knew without a doubt he wanted her. Just as fiercely, just as primitively, as she wanted him. He kissed her hungrily, moving against her with coaxing, then demanding, urgent, restless movements.

And she kissed him back, wanting to savor the moment, wanting it to last, wanting to carry the memory of it into another life.

Stone was stunned to feel himself losing it as her hands rushed over him, pulling him closer. His control was unraveling, the need tearing at him until he was ready to ignore the fact that she'd just been released from the hospital. All he could think of was being buried in the heat and softness of her, over and over and over again until morning.

Hot, driving need made his hands impatient, his mouth hungry and demanding as their hands slowly rediscovered and aroused, under cover of darkness. But in full view of the moon and the stars high above them.

Then reason kicked in. Dahlia had been in a coma for thirty-six hours. She'd been in the hospital for a week. And they hadn't slept in the same bed for months.

Or made love in…forever, it seemed.

Stone reluctantly dragged his mouth from hers, his hunger a dull ache and unsatisfied. He looked carefully into her eyes. The blue gaze was drugged with desire, mildly surprised that he'd pulled away and slightly irritated that he'd stopped kissing her.

His relief was profound. *This* was the Dahlia he'd married—not the prim, calm and serene person she'd been all week in the hospital. Or in the car this morning.

"What do you say we make our excuses to everyone and go upstairs?" Stone suggested, pulling her back into his arms where she belonged. "Or, better yet," he said, his voice low and soft against her ear, "let's skip the excuses and make a run for it."

Her cheek felt silky smooth when he kissed it lightly.

"Where?" Dahlia turned her face so he could kiss her mouth, and her arms tightened around his neck.

"Where?" Stone was distracted by the button on her shirt that had come undone, giving him a better view of her creamy, tantalizing breasts.

"Where do you want to go?" she asked and then kissed his throat, the tip of her tongue tracing a little path downward to where his shirt was buttoned.

"To our room, of course."

Dahlia lifted her head, her blue gaze locking suddenly on his. "To our room?" She stepped back and stared up at him. "What…what are you saying?"

Stone grew still. He felt as though he'd been slam-dunked into cold reality. This was no time for thinking, and he sighed heavily as he tried to come up with a response. Making love would not solve their problems, but he couldn't see how separate bedrooms were getting them anywhere—except farther apart.

"I'm hoping it can mean a fresh start," he answered slowly, truthfully. But his hopes were dashed when he saw her frown in consternation.

"I can't." She stared up at him, looking suddenly tired and alone and very confused.

Stone took pity on her, tamping back his desire. And his frustration. But this was as close as he'd been to her in months and he didn't want it to end.

"You look exhausted," he told her bluntly. "I shouldn't have agreed to the party tonight, but Rocky and Field insisted, and Blade backed them up. Said it would do you good to know how much they care about you."

How much they cared? Dahlia felt a sharp, piercing pain shooting through her heart.

But Stone drew the back of his fingers down the side of her face, leaving a light trail of goose bumps. The sudden compassion in his eyes undermined her defenses. She didn't want him looking at her like that, with eyes as gray as a thundercloud, glimmering with sympathy and maybe more—with shared loss.

It was too late for that. Too late for sharing or wanting or needing anything from him. Emotionally she wasn't ready. And she certainly didn't want to make promises she knew she couldn't keep. It wouldn't be fair to Stone. Not when she'd be joining Brooke soon.

But, she had to admit, her earlier reaction to Stone still rattled her.

In her head.

In her gut.

Oh dear, even down to her toes. And she wondered suddenly if angels *could* make love.

As Dahlia stood there, hollowed-out and afloat, she floundered for direction. She struggled to stay focused on her mission to restore Stone's faith. To make him believe in himself, in his son and all the good things in life.

But it was too late for the two of them.

It was much too late. No matter how good it had felt to

hold him and kiss him and feel desire tearing through her, she was still an angel on a mission. And she must, by all that she held dear, try to act like one.

"I'm an angel," she stated suddenly, softly. And not a very good one either, she added silently to herself. "Basil sent me here to help you."

A small sigh escaped him. "Honey, you're tired—"

"Don't you believe me, Stone?" Their gazes met and held.

"I believe that's what you believe," he told her slowly.

Dahlia was disappointed. "But you don't believe in angels or…or anything, do you?"

"I believe you sustained a severe blow to the head that put you in a coma for almost two days." His voice was low and ragged. "I believe you saw something that made you think you were in…that made you believe…"

"You can't even say it, can you?" she asked him gently. "I was in heaven, Stone. Or, at least at the gate. And I saw her," Dahlia burst out. "I saw Brooke."

Stone grew still. "Don't say that to me," he began in a voice as hard as it was even.

"Don't you believe Brooke went to heaven?"

"Yes, of course I do," he said in a burst of frustration. "But you didn't see her because she's dead. We buried her—you and I—twelve months ago. Brooke is in the cemetery with both my parents and my grandparents. You had a dream, just a coma-induced dream, damn it!"

Dahlia smiled bittersweetly. "You shouldn't swear at an angel."

Dahlia was driving him nuts.

Weren't things bad enough without her adding flights of fancy to an already difficult situation?

He sighed and reluctantly released her.

He knew Dahlia couldn't help what she felt—or what

she believed. He recalled that one of the doctors thought that believing she was an angel was Dahlia's way of dealing with her grief.

And it was about time she did deal with it, he knew. For the past year, she'd behaved as though nothing had changed. When everything had.

"Good night, Stone."

Stone felt her keen disappointment in him. Sensed how badly she wanted him to believe she was some heavenly creature sent from above to help him.

"Good night, Dahlia."

His gaze followed her as she slipped around the side of the house. And he wondered if it wasn't too late for the two of them.

Wandering through the rose garden alone, his mind traveled back over the past year, slamming into each of the stumbling blocks he'd put directly in Dahlia's path—and he started to swear.

Silently, vividly, coldly.

His gaze traveled upstairs to where he saw a light come on in Brooke's room. The room Dahlia had fled to months ago, when his silence had driven her away. He'd never meant to drive her out of their bedroom. Never intended for her to be lonely or unhappy.

But it was hard, so very hard, to love a child—and then lose her.

Stone knew part of him had died with Brooke.

He also realized now, tonight, what a fool he'd been to put his marriage at risk—and he made a silent vow to get Dahlia back.

Chapter Three

Stone was loading the last of the fencing into the back of the pickup truck the next morning, when he heard a burst of laughter behind him. He turned and saw Dahlia and the two children trooping down the front steps. As they passed him, they all merrily waved, but kept on going.

"Hey, where you off to?" he asked curiously.

Dahlia stopped and raised the picnic basket she was carrying. "On a picnic, of course."

Stone frowned. He felt foolish, keeping tabs on her, but he was equally certain she was not up to this. "You got out of the hospital yesterday. You shouldn't be walking around in the hot sun," he stated flatly, surprised at how harsh he sounded.

Some of the joy seemed to go out of the group.

"I'm in the shade," Dahlia said, touching her wide-brimmed straw hat. "And there's a nice breeze. We're going to gather wildflowers and go wading in the stream."

Stone hesitated. Dahlia looked too good to be in the medical condition he knew she was in. She was slim and tanned in a sleeveless white shirt and denim shorts. She looked healthy enough, but Stone knew she wasn't.

"I think I'll come along. I could use a break," he added lightly.

Both Dahlia and Field looked rather stunned, which sent a shot of pain through him. Had it been that long since he'd been on a picnic with his family?

Stone sent the truckload of materials to the area where the ranch hands were mending fences, with a message to Blade that he had something else he had to do. He fell in beside Dahlia and took the picnic basket out of her hand.

It was a bright, sunny Saturday morning, and Stone was glad he'd decided to come with them. Field and Shannon chased each other, laughing and talking, and it struck him suddenly that he hadn't heard his son laugh in a very long time.

And when the children fell in step beside them, Shannon talked to Dahlia endlessly, as though she were a sponge, soaking up every ounce of attention for some future time when she'd be suffering a drought. Not for the first time, Stone noticed that Dahlia was good with children.

She had such deep respect for a child. Any child. No one suspected she was Field's stepmother, and those who knew she wasn't his biological mother had nearly forgotten it by now.

Dahlia was a natural-born mother. A voice inside him taunted, *Remember what she used to say about filling up the house with lots of little Tylers?*

But you're standing in her way, cowboy.

Stone winced, but he told his inner voice to go to hell. He couldn't bring another child into this world. He wasn't even sure what to do with the one he had left.

He stole a look at Field. Sometimes he wondered if he

was doing the right thing, sending his remaining child away to school, especially when Field clearly didn't want to go.

But what else could he do?

It was more important for Field to be safe, than it was for him to be happy. At least for the next few years. Until he was older. Maybe then...

Stone trudged down the path that led to the stream, feeling alone and empty and more than a little disgruntled.

When they reached the shaded bank of the stream, the children tore off their shoes and socks and jumped in, squealing with delight. Stone set the basket on the ground and watched them as they splashed each other, his thoughts sober.

"A penny for your thoughts." Dahlia stood at his side, her head tipped back so she could see him.

He glanced at her, his grin fleeting. "They're not worth that much."

"Oh yeah? Try me."

He shrugged. "I was just thinking of all those times I came out here to go wading when I was a kid. The sun was hot, the water was cold, and it just felt so good to be alive."

"It can still be that way, Stone, if you'd give yourself a chance."

Her words were gentle, but they only made him angry. With her—but mostly with himself.

"How can an angel give me advice on feeling the joy of being alive?" he asked her bluntly, his voice low and tight with frustration. He had her this time, he thought with bittersweet satisfaction. She wouldn't be able to give him an answer.

"I'm only trying to—"

"Help me. Yeah, I've heard that already." He sighed and looked directly at her. She was so beautiful standing there in the sun-splattered shade, the wide-brimmed straw hat making her look no older than a teenager. "Just out of curiosity, can you feel the sun on your arms and smell the mountain cedar?"

Dahlia nodded. "Of course."

"I thought angels weren't supposed to feel anything like the rest of us mortals," he said. Man, was he in a bad mood this morning. It came from no sleep, and missing Dahlia. And it all seemed so damned hopeless in the clear light of day.

"Stone, I don't have all the answers." She touched his arm with one slim hand. "All I know is what I told you in the hospital and again last night. Basil—"

"Who is this Basil you keep mentioning?" he said impatiently.

"Uh...um." Dahlia bit her lower lip and tried not to wince when she said, "He's the chief angel."

"The chief angel," Stone repeated.

"I think so, yes."

"Don't you know?" This had to be the most ridiculous—

"I know he's in charge of letting people through the gate," she informed him seriously.

He had her now, Stone gloated. "You said people, not angels," he pointed out to her.

Dahlia frowned. "I...I think I won't be a real angel until I walk through the gate and down the path to get my halo."

"Your halo?"

"I have a ticket to get one. And wings, too."

Stone sobered quickly, his joy at tripping her up vanishing completely. Because she was so serious, so intent, that he knew in a flash that she believed everything she was saying.

And it scared the living hell out of him.

Somewhere deep inside, he had been hoping that Dahlia

was just a little...confused. And that it would go away in time.

But it wasn't going away.

It was getting worse. Much worse.

"I think I'm sort of an angel-in-training," Dahlia was saying.

"An angel-in-training?"

She nodded earnestly. "I have to complete my mission—maybe it's a test—but anyway, if I get it right, then I can go back and be with Brooke."

Stone stepped toward her and took off her wide-brimmed hat. She watched him as he drew her gently, carefully, into his arms. He wanted to crush her to him, to hold on to her tightly so she wouldn't slip farther away from him—but he couldn't.

She was too delicate, too fragile.

"You don't believe a word I said, do you?" Dahlia accused with her nose pressed against his throat. She sounded profoundly disappointed in him.

"Honey, Brooke's dead." Stone spoke softly, but he wanted to shout it from the top of the nearest mountain. "She's dead."

"Don't you think I know that? I saw her."

Oh, damn. Damn! He tightened his arms around her. The doctors were right. Dahlia was using this angel business to cope with Brooke's death, to maintain a connection with her.

Dahlia still felt a lot of guilt—unfounded to be sure—but it was there nonetheless, strong and powerful and wearing on her soul.

Because she'd been busy making pickles and hadn't noticed that Brooke had slipped out to go for an unsupervised morning ride on Firelight. Dahlia thought Brooke had merely wanted to say good-morning to her horse, before returning to straighten up her room.

By the time Dahlia realized Brooke hadn't returned to the house, their daughter had ridden Firelight into the meadow along the river.

And by the time they found Brooke…she was already dead.

This mission to help him was merely Dahlia's way of making some misguided retribution for what she thought she'd done to their lives.

Stone drew her closer and swallowed hard. Resting his chin on her soft hair, he gazed out at the streaks of water glinting brightly in the sun. The water rushed over the rocks where the children were playing, laughing and shouting, but all he heard was the roaring in his ears.

Because it was his fault Brooke had died. He never should have given her a horse like Firelight until she was at least twelve. She wasn't a boy, but a little girl, small and delicate and only seven years old. She wasn't strong enough or big enough or old enough to handle a mare like Firelight.

Dahlia pulled away enough to look up at him. Tears sparkled in her huge smoky blue eyes. "Please…please let me help you so I can see Brooke again."

Stone would have given her anything right then. "What do you want from me?"

"Let Field stay here on the ranch. Don't send him away."

Stone struggled to regain his emotional footing. Dahlia was so determined. And so heart-twistingly vulnerable. "Anything but that." He spoke slowly, then winced inside when he saw the anxiety in her eyes build to sheer panic.

She tried to step back, away from him. Stone had every

intention of releasing her, but his arms tightened instead of loosening. He couldn't let her go. Not yet.

He savored the feel of her, the softness and the warmth. She was flesh and blood and heart and soul. She was no angel—but who wanted an angel for a wife, anyway?

Finally, Stone had no choice but to let go of her. Not only because of the two children playing near them. But mostly because he couldn't take all the things he needed from her without giving her what she needed from him, and it was impossible for him to do that.

He knew she wanted another child—and he couldn't let her have one. He couldn't allow himself to have another one.

Dahlia wanted Field to remain on the ranch instead of living away at boarding school—and that was impossible, too.

And, oh yeah, she wanted him to open up to her, to talk to her, to spill his guts to her. Because what Dahlia wanted the most was for him to talk to her about his feelings.

Especially his feelings about Brooke's accident.

But he couldn't do that, either.

He had to be strong. He had to protect the family he loved. He had to guide them in the right direction and keep them safe. And he couldn't protect them by spouting off about something he couldn't change. It would only upset them.

And besides…all the talking in the world wasn't going to bring his little girl back.

With a deep and unsteady breath, Stone let his hands fall to his sides. Their future remained an enormous question mark, but if he gave in to Dahlia, he knew what the future would hold for them. More pain. More tragedy. And a lot more heartbreak.

''I'm doing this for you!'' he blurted out as though she'd

been arguing with him. "For us! For our family! This is not a safe place to raise a child."

"Your father raised the four of you on this ranch," she gently reminded him.

"Yeah, and we made it to adulthood by some miracle!" Stone retorted.

It was obviously Dahlia's turn to gloat. "Maybe someone was watching out for all of you even back then," she said, her half smile making him even more frustrated.

"I meant, my brothers and I repeatedly found ourselves in dangerous situations." He hit every syllable as though his life depended upon making her understand.

And it did. His life. And her life.

But more to the point—his son's life.

"There are countless dangers for a child on a ranch," Stone continued relentlessly. "Swimming in the river after a hard rain. Getting in the way when we're breaking a colt or herding sheep. Fishing, rock climbing, canoeing, hiking, camping—damn it, just wandering all over the ranch without supervision is enough danger all by itself!"

"If you explain to Field that he has to stay out of the way, that he can't go wandering off until he's older—"

"That won't fix it," Stone sharply cut her off. He watched the children playing in the stream, resisting the urge to make them stop.

Field was intensely interested in the day-to-day workings of the ranch, he knew. The kid was destined to be a rancher. It was in his blood, in his heart, and until the day that Brooke died, Stone had been pleased by his son's eagerness to grow up and be like him.

But he wanted more for his son than backbreaking work in the hot Texas sun. Or to compete in dangerous rodeo events for fun—even if it was for charity. Not all Tyler men were cut out for ranching. Flint wasn't. His younger brother had followed his own path, blazed his own trail, into an academic career.

But shouldn't Field have the right to blaze his own trail? a voice demanded deep inside Stone. Even if that trail leads straight back to this ranch?

Or—God forbid—a career on the pro rodeo circuit?

Stone studied his son, who was jumping from rock to rock as he crossed the stream with his cousin. He wasn't blind to how deeply Field loved it here on the ranch. Or how much the boy loved the sheep and the horses and the dogs. Or just the sheer freedom of living in this wide-open country.

Stone had grown up with the same deep feelings for this place. And for this life.

But as he watched the slim figure of his only surviving child make it safely to the opposite bank, he breathed easier. Was having personal freedom ever worth the price of a child's life?

No, of course not.

"You have to start believing in Field," Dahlia said quietly, softly, *gently,* as though he were the child and not Field. "You have to start believing in yourself and your ability to take care of him."

Stone looked at her. "But I can't take care of him," he said with blunt honesty. "I can't keep him safe. I can't keep him whole or emotionally sound. All I can do is make the best decisions I know how to make—and hope to God Field forgives me when he grows up."

Then he turned and walked away, following the path downstream.

Dahlia wanted to scream at him to come back, to yell at him for being so stubborn and pigheaded and so...so filled with guilt over Brooke's death that he couldn't see straight.

But she couldn't. Because she was an angel.

But maybe...

Dahlia ran after him. "If I can prove to you that I'm an angel and not just crazy because of the bump on my head, then will you reconsider sending Field away?"

Stone stopped and turned slowly around to face her. "What kind of proof did you have in mind?" he asked warily. "Snow in August? Or maybe you can summon a twister. It's a little late in the year for one, so what if I make it easier on you? How about whipping us up a hurricane. Yeah, a hurricane in August."

"August and September are the traditional months for hurricanes in Texas," Dahlia absently replied. How could she prove it to him? Thinking hard, she turned slowly around until her gaze landed on the children.

They were crossing back and forth over the stream on the wide flat rocks embedded in the water, giggling as the shallow rapids splashed their bare feet. Dahlia glanced once toward heaven and silently prayed, Please, Basil, help me convince him. Then, taking a deep breath, she concentrated on making a miracle happen. To her joy and considerable surprise, a large, lovely rainbow appeared in the sunlight among the rocks.

Her prayers had been answered!

"Do you see it?" she cried happily.

"I see a rainbow, not the heavenly gate." Stone sounded cross and Dahlia thought perhaps she'd sounded a bit too proud of herself.

"But I did it! A rainbow, and it hasn't been raining!" She couldn't help it. She'd produced a rainbow out of thin air and the power had gone to her head. "I did it!"

"A rainbow is caused by the reflection and refraction of the sun's rays as they fall on drops of water," Stone informed her stiffly. "And you don't need rain for a rainbow.

I was in Niagara Falls once on a sunny day and saw a rainbow in the spray from the falls.''

Okay, Mr. Smarty-pants. Dahlia frowned, turned her attention to the rainbow and concentrated fiercely. Basil, please, she begged, and held her breath.

As she fastened her gaze on the rainbow, the colors intensified.

"There, do you see it?"

Stone shrugged, but she noticed he didn't take his eyes off the rainbow that was growing more beautiful with each passing second. Both children had noticed it, too, and they were standing like statues in the middle of the stream, gazing at the rainbow as though it were a gift from God.

And it was. Dahlia knew that for a fact.

"It's a pretty rainbow," was all Stone said. Then he added, "But if you really want to convince me, plop down a pot of gold at one end of it. I could sure use the cash."

Just then Field shouted, "Look what I found! Mom! Dad! Look!"

Their son came rushing toward them, carrying something in his hand. Shannon was right behind him.

"He found it at the end of the rainbow!"

"A gold nugget, Dad! Look, Mom—gold!"

The children were jumping up and down in excitement, both chattering at once. It took a moment for Stone and Dahlia to see what Field held in the palm of his hand. It was, indeed, a gold nugget, about the size of a grape.

The children raced off to look for more gold.

"I said a pot of gold, not a lump," Stone growled when her eyes met his.

"What do you expect? I'm only an angel-in-training."

"And I looked down and there it was!" Field announced importantly at dinner that night.

"You think this is worth anything?" Rocky said to no one in particular, as he passed it to Flint.

"I've never heard of much gold mining in Texas," Blade put in. "South Dakota, yeah. And California. But not Texas."

"It could be an alluvial deposit," Flint said.

"It's a gold nugget," Field told his uncle.

Flint smiled. "Nuggets of gold are washed and carried away from the vein, or source of the gold, by surface water. Alluvial deposits of gold are far away from the vein, usually found in stream beds."

"Then you think it's the real thing?" Blade asked doubtfully, frowning.

"Probably not." Flint bounced the nugget in the palm of his hand for an instant, then passed it to its owner. Looking at the disappointment on his nephew's face, he added, "But it's possible."

Stone placed his knife and fork on his plate, grateful to Flint for the shining happiness in his son's eyes. He, too, hadn't had the heart to tell Field the nugget was probably a piece of pyrite, or fool's gold.

Stone was also grateful that Blade hadn't spoken up. His older brother was a kind and gentle man, but he was also one to call a spade a spade—even to a ten-year-old child.

Stone sipped his lemonade and listened to the two children's conversation. Six-year-old Shannon offered every suggestion she could think of about how Field should spend his newfound fortune, but Stone wasn't worried. Field merely listened to each suggestion and shook his head vehemently. "I'm going to keep it always," he announced.

It was good, Stone thought, for a boy to keep some of his dreams alive. And what was the point of stampeding all over Field's joy by explaining the nugget wasn't true gold? Field was much too young for a dose of that kind of reality. He'd already had Santa Claus and the Easter Bunny taken away from him, although Stone and Dahlia had tried to prolong those particular fantasies for as long as possible.

But they hadn't been able to keep the most important childhood fantasy intact, Stone thought helplessly. The fantasy that a boy's father would always be able to protect his children and keep them safe. No matter what.

Brooke's death had sent that fantasy spinning in the wind.

Stone stole a glance at Dahlia, who was sitting at the opposite end of the table, watching Field with a warm smile. Wearing a white sundress, her spun gold hair combed into a loose chignon for coolness, she looked so elegant and graceful and so heartbreakingly pure, Stone's breath caught in his throat.

He was reminded of the first time he'd met her. She'd been wearing a white dress that day, too. Her hair had been even longer back then, and it had been tied back with a blue silk scarf that had matched her eyes perfectly. And she'd smelled like flowers.

Like an angel would smell.

Stone's heart skipped a beat. Where had that blasted rainbow come from? And the nugget of gold—just the right angelic touch, he sighed, his thoughts turning cynical. Maybe it was dead wrong to allow Field to believe that worthless lump of shining metal was something real.

Getting a good education was real. And working hard—that was real, too.

But angels weren't.

"Mom? Can I come in?" The voice at her bedroom door sounded anxious.

Dahlia called, "Of course!" She set aside the magazine

she'd been flipping through and looked expectantly toward the door.

Field, dressed in worn jeans and a bright blue T-shirt, launched himself across the room and onto the bed with her. "Oops. Did I bounce too much?"

Dahlia smiled and put her arm around him. "You bounced just right."

They snuggled on Brooke's twin canopy bed, leaning on the pillows propped against the headboard. For a long time, Dahlia didn't think Field was going to say anything. But then he did. "This bed's dumb."

"Dumb?" She was surprised. "What's dumb about it?"

"That ruffly thing overhead."

She laughed. "Girls like ruffles. And lots of them."

"Brooke didn't."

"She liked her bed…including that *ruffly thing*." Dahlia rumpled his thick dark hair affectionately.

She sat quietly, giving him a chance to talk about his sister if he wanted to. Field had been a little over two years old when Brooke was born. And she remembered the way he'd always looked out for her, searching for hours for the favorite teddy bear she'd misplaced. Or patiently playing a "sissy" game with her on a rainy afternoon.

Not that they hadn't had their share of fights. Dahlia smiled at the memory of days of endless teasing between her children.

"She was so many people," Field said.

"She was?"

"Yeah. You know, one minute she'd be lining up those dumb bears of hers—and me, too—to teach us how to draw and paint.…"

Dahlia grinned. "Those famous art classes of hers."

"And the next she'd be punching my arm 'cause I stole

one of the bears' cookies," Field complained wistfully. "I never knew what to expect from her."

"Brooke taught you a valuable lesson."

Field tilted his head back so he could look at her. "She did?"

Dahlia nodded. "Never get overconfident when dealing with a woman."

Field continued to stare blankly up at her.

She laughed and dropped a kiss on the top of his head. Field merely blinked once and frowned in confusion. "You'll understand better when you start dating," she said.

That got the expected response. "Mom...oh ma-an..." And then a muttered "Yuk."

Dahlia sighed in contentment. She noticed Field was holding something protectively in his hand, and she patiently waited for him to show it to her. It was his lump of gold, and Dahlia asked curiously, "What are you going to do with it?"

"Save it forever," he answered promptly.

Lately, Field saved everything. Little treasures he'd picked up around the ranch, some mementos of Brooke and a few things that had once belonged to other members of the family.

Like the knife Rocky had given him. The one that had once belonged to Stone. Field was never without it, and Dahlia knew the knife was inside his pocket at this very moment. She'd seen the bulge in his back pocket when she'd hugged him.

It was as though Field was snatching at anything tangible—items he could touch and hold in his own two hands—because those he loved were slipping away from him. Dahlia felt tears threaten and she swallowed hard.

Field had already lost his sister and all semblance of the home life he was accustomed to. If Stone followed through and made the child attend boarding school during the week, then Field would lose all his friends and classmates he'd started first grade with in Lemon Falls.

And he was about to lose her, as well.

If she completed her mission, she'd have to leave him in order to be with Brooke in heaven.

"Mom? You okay?"

Dahlia was far from being okay, but she smiled at him. And breathed in the little-boy smell of him, trying desperately to imprint the scent of bubble gum, freshly washed cotton and chocolate bars in her memory bank. Along with the faint smell of the barn and the stables.

"I'm fine, sweetie. What about you? Did you check on Ginger?" One of their herding dogs, the full-size russet and white collie was due to give birth within the next week or so.

Field nodded as he pocketed his lump of gold. "I sat with her, and she put her head in my lap. Mom, could I...do you think, maybe...?"

"What?" she asked gently.

Familiar gray eyes looked into hers. "Could I have one of the puppies?"

Dahlia sucked in a breath. She now understood the reason for this evening visit. Blade was planning to sell half of Ginger's puppies to neighboring sheep ranches, to be trained as herding dogs. Expensive herding dogs. And the other half were to be raised and trained on the Tyler ranch. As working dogs. Not as pets.

"I want a puppy of my own. To raise it and take care of it—"

"I'll see what I can do," she broke in, her voice gentle with understanding. He wanted something of his very own to love. "Let's wait and see how many puppies Ginger has, and then I'll speak to your dad."

The light that had flashed briefly in his eyes quickly died when she mentioned Stone. And she heard Field mutter, "Then what's the use?"

"Field—"

"He'll just say no." Field's voice was low and resentful and terribly, terribly hurt.

"Sweetie, your dad—"

"What did I do, Mom?" He looked up at her in honest bewilderment. "What did I do that was bad enough to be sent away?"

"Honey…"

But Field was scrambling off the bed. "Good night, Mom."

"Field, wait!" But the door had already closed behind him.

What was she supposed to do now? How could she walk away from the torment in her son's eyes? How could she do that and still call herself a loving mother? If only Stone…

But Stone was in a prison of his own pain, locking everyone else out. It would take a miracle for her to help the two people she loved most in this world.

And she was fresh out.

Dahlia's gaze landed on the photograph of Brooke on the night table. She picked it up and hugged it to herself, hurting for both of her children.

And she tried to forget that time was quickly running out.

Chapter Four

"But I don't want to go." Field's voice was low as he kept his eyes on the kitchen floor.

Stone was on one knee in front of his small son so they could be at eye level with each other. He said gently, "Once you see the school, your fears will—"

"I'm not scared!" Field burst out in angry denial, yanking his head up so he could look directly into his father's eyes. "I just don't want to go," he said in a more polite tone of voice. Then in a more pleading one, "I want to stay here with you and Mom."

Stone sighed roughly and swallowed past the mass of pain that was lodged in his throat. Frustration strained in him like a dog against its chain. "We have to get you registered, Field. We should have done that before, only…"

His voice trailed off. Stone was all too aware of Dahlia standing by the central island, watching them. Field would have been registered in school by now if not for her accident.

Or the series of emergencies that had kept him from driving into San Antonio. He'd been trying since Monday to get Field registered, but one thing after another had kept him tied to the ranch this past week.

A lost lamb, fencing and machinery to repair, various problems with the Jeeps and trucks, and lost car keys. All reasonable, everyday things that happened all the time on a spread this size.

But not all at once.

Stone glanced briefly at Dahlia.

And not when he was racing against time to get Field into this particular boarding school.

Stone had contacted the school two months ago and secured a position for his son to start fifth grade in the fall. But they wouldn't hold the position open indefinitely without Field being properly registered. Stone had received a letter last week saying as much.

He returned his attention to the small, forlorn little boy standing before him. Tension radiated from the child, his feet spread wide, fists nailed to his sides, and Stone could see he was angrily fighting back tears.

An unearthly shot of pain splintered through Stone. "It's a good school," he said patiently. "Lots of trees and green lawns. A lot of kids your own age to play with. You'll eat in the same dining hall with them and have a roommate. It'll be fun. Before you know it, it'll seem like home to you...."

Stone let his words trail off, knowing how lame he'd sounded. How totally ineffectual. Boarding school wasn't at all like home. But he had to convince Field everything would be all right.

"You know how much you love it in San Antonio," Stone continued with forced cheerfulness. "Uncle Flint and Shannon will only be a few minutes away." He waited, but there was still no reaction, not one glimmer of interest. There was only sadness in his son's eyes that pierced Stone's heart.

"Come on, give it a chance," he urged. "At least visit the school and let's see how you feel then."

Hope flared in the boy's eyes. "And if I don't like it, do I still have to go?"

Damn! "Give me a break here, Field." Stone was losing patience fast. But mostly with himself. "You're not giving the school a chance. You're prepared to dislike it before—" Stone stopped when Field nodded vigorously. "What are you agreeing to? That you're not going to like this school no matter what?"

Field nodded again, more hesitantly this time, as he warily watched his father.

"Answer me." Stone's voice remained low and patient.

"I won't like any school away from home."

His son might not have Dahlia's blood running through his veins, but he definitely had her sense of logic. He regarded his son with a mixture of love and respect for his feelings—and the sheer, blunt, all-consuming need to keep him safe.

No matter what the cost.

That last sentiment had a stranglehold on Stone, and he knew it all too well. But he couldn't get free of it. And, truthfully, he didn't want to be free of it.

The risk to Field was just too great.

The most important thing a father could give his children was security. To protect them from danger. He hadn't done that with Brooke and now she was dead.

He wouldn't make the same mistake with his only remaining child.

But it hurt Stone to see the sadness in his son's eyes, and he very nearly relented. He knew the joy of growing up out here in the hill country. Exploring caves and spending sun-filled hours fishing and thinking and dreaming about the future. Of moonlight rides along the banks of the river. He knew the joy of sheer space that only growing up on a ranch could provide.

But Stone also knew the savage, never-ending pain of losing a child. Life on a ranch was a double-edged sword. All that joy and space and freedom didn't mean squat when you had to put a seven-year-old in the ground and say goodbye to her forever.

He slowly straightened. "It's time to go." He held out his hand toward Field, then let it drop to his side when his son merely turned and walked out the door. They could hear his footsteps as he crossed the dining room, the front hall, and then walked out the front door. The screen door closed softly behind him.

Dahlia gathered up her purse, looked at him and said gently, "I believe that's the first time I've ever seen Field refuse to take your hand."

Stone flinched. He watched her walk ahead of him, following their son out the door. He found this new angelic Dahlia to be much more frustrating than the opinionated, outspoken, hot-blooded woman he'd married years ago.

Oh, Lord, was he now losing his mind on top of everything else? He must be, because that was the only explanation for even thinking about the possibility that Dahlia could be an angel!

It was a silent ride toward San Antonio and Stone didn't know how much more he could take. But as they approached Lemon Falls, the town closest to the ranch, he quickly discovered that he'd have to learn to take a lot more. A whole lot more.

Because he discovered his new Explorer had a flat tire.

And so did the spare.

Stone swore soundly beneath his breath, aware of Dahlia and Field getting out of the car to see what was wrong.

"These tires are new!" Stone exploded. "Six months old! This one shouldn't be flat, and neither should the spare! It's...it's *impossible!*"

"Maybe someone's trying to tell you something," Dahlia murmured softly, for his ears alone.

Stone glared angrily at her, and her smile turned into such a mischievous grin that all thought went right out of his head. Her blue eyes sparkled like diamonds and she looked so happy and pretty in the warm sunshine that his anger vanished.

"I suppose now you're going to take credit for this little episode," he said mildly.

Dahlia ignored him. But Stone's gaze slowly took in Field, who was standing silently off to one side, sheer undisguised relief in his gray eyes.

Stone turned his attention back to the spare tire, and carefully ran his fingers over it until he felt the ragged slash. He glanced at Field, who was watching him. And when their eyes met, Stone was startled at the quick way Field dropped his gaze.

Rage filled him instantly, replaced almost immediately with shock and sadness at what he was thinking.

Stone started to lock up the car. "We'll have to hike into town and get Trey to send someone out here with a couple of new tires," he said calmly, reining in his temper with an effort. Trey Daniels owned the garage and gas station in Lemon Falls, and was a high school buddy.

In a few minutes the three of them were headed toward town, with Field wandering ahead of them, happily skipping and jumping and whistling under his breath. And Stone's sigh was heavy.

"Look at it this way," Dahlia said to him. "You've made a little boy very happy this morning."

"I didn't make him happy. Those damned flat tires did," he pointed out. "And don't for one minute think this is the end of it, because it isn't. We'll get some lunch in town while the guys get the Explorer fixed up and ready to go. And then you and I are going to take Field into San Antonio…and get him registered. There's still plenty of time."

"I thought you had things you had to do this afternoon," Dahlia reminded him.

Stone looked at her. "It'll keep," he said flatly. "But I'm getting Field registered at that school if it's the last thing I do today—witches and angels and ghosts and imps, notwithstanding."

She merely smiled up at him.

"Damn it, Dahlia, how could you let that happen?" he demanded as they trudged along together. Field's low, happy whistling was making Stone irritable.

"Are you saying I had something to do with those two flat tires?"

"I wouldn't put it past you, with the mood you're in lately," he muttered.

"But, Stone, I didn't think you believed in the power of angels," she said, gazing up at him hopefully.

"I believe in the power of a sharp instrument applied to two perfectly good tires!"

"Then you think I…I stabbed those perfectly harmless little tires in order to keep you from taking Field into San Antonio?"

Stone stared ahead at Field. "Someone did a number on those tires," he said, his gaze narrowing thoughtfully. He didn't want to believe it, but—

Dahlia grabbed him by the sleeve, pulling him to a stop

beside her. "Are you saying you think Field punctured the tires?" Her eyes were wide with shock and disbelief.

"He carries that knife with him all the time."

"But, Stone—"

"Someone deliberately slashed the spare and put a tiny cut into the other one, so all the air would leak out and we'd end up stranded out here for a while," he said quietly. "We're lucky we're only a couple of miles from town. We could have easily ended up stranded halfway between the ranch and Lemon Falls."

"But to think your own son—"

"I'm sure it was on impulse. He didn't want to go, he saw the tires and he had the knife."

"What did you mean a moment ago when you asked how I could let this happen?" Dahlia asked him slowly.

Stone's sigh was weary. "I only meant that if you'd back me up about boarding school, Field wouldn't get it in his head that he could get away with stunts like this one."

"I can't back you up when I think you're wrong," she said so softly that Stone had to strain to hear her.

He shrugged helplessly and started walking. Dahlia fell into step beside him. After a moment or two of tense, uneasy silence, he gently asked her, "Why is it so important to you that I let Field go to school in Lemon Falls this year?"

Dahlia waited a moment before she replied. "I don't want anything to come between the two of you. Especially now," she added softly.

Dahlia's gaze wandered to where their son was pretending to be an airplane, his arms making flying motions as he walked far ahead of them.

"Remember how we used to talk about raising our children?" she said. "We wanted to give them every advantage of growing up on a ranch, with plenty of freedom within a safe environment—"

"But it's not safe, damn it!" Stone growled.

"Stone, you can't always protect the people you love." Again she spoke in that soft voice of reason that grated on his nerves. "Field loves it on the ranch. I don't want you to send him away, because if you do, you're going to ruin your relationship with him. You're hurting him," she said over his sputtering protests, "and I can't stand to watch it. He thinks you're punishing him by sending him away."

"Punishing him?" That thought had never entered Stone's mind. "Did he tell you that?"

"Not exactly. He wanted to know what he'd done that was so bad that he had to be sent away."

Stone groaned inwardly. If only he could get Dahlia and Field to understand. "I'll talk to him. Explain…"

"Words mean nothing to a child. But actions do. Stone, he needs you. He's hurting and he misses—"

"Don't say it. Don't suggest that I'm rejecting my son by wanting what's best for him."

Dahlia hugged herself as though she were cold, despite the bright, hot sun. "It's your rejection of the life you used to enjoy that hurts him, Stone. You've shut yourself off from your own son. You've become hard and controlling and act as though Field's feelings mean absolutely nothing to you."

Stone started to speak, then saw the lone tear rolling slowly down her cheek. The fat tear sparkled in the sunlight and made it impossible for him to utter a sound.

Dahlia didn't notice. Not his stiff silence and not the fact that she was quietly crying. A second tear had escaped, slid down her face and splashed to the ground.

"You're his father," she stated flatly, staring straight ahead. "You need to be there for him to talk to and listen

when he has a problem. You need to let him ride his horse.
You need to let him do all the things he did before Brooke
died. He needs you and you need him. If you send him
away now, when he needs you the most, you'll lose him
forever. Is that what you want?''

Dahlia jerked her head around suddenly to face him.
"Well, is it?''

"No.'' No, damn it, that wasn't what he wanted.

He wanted Field to be happy.

But he also wanted him to be safe.

How could he let his son continue to ride Gray Cloud
all over the ranch? How could he, after what had happened
to his daughter?

Dahlia brushed her hand across her face, fingers rubbing
away her tears in an impatient gesture. "You were always
such a good father, Stone,'' she said wearily. "The night
we met, Field was all you talked about. You were very
young and alone, with all the responsibilities of a single
father, and yet you thought raising your son was so cool. I
remember one night you called home a half-dozen times
during dinner because he had a cold. That's when I fell
in—'' Dahlia broke off, snatching the words back.

Stone's heart started racing, knowing what she had been
about to say. She'd fallen in love with him, a mere day and
a half after they met.

But he'd fallen in love with her the instant he saw her.

And now look at them. Separated by a world of pain and
grief.

"You're a nurturing man. Who spent most of last evening anxiously pacing the barn waiting for Ginger to give
birth to her nine puppies?'' Dahlia sent him a smile.

But Stone suddenly flashed on Brooke, the way she'd
held on to his finger with a tight little fist the first few
months of her life. He remembered the way she used to

look trustingly up at him, knowing he'd always protect her and keep her from harm.

Dahlia thought he'd been a good father?

A good father, a nurturing father, would not have given his seven-year-old daughter a horse of her own! Stone shifted uncomfortably at the thought.

He wanted to yell it in Field's ear to make him understand.

And he wanted to do whatever it took to make Dahlia understand why he was doing all this!

Instead, Stone set a brisk pace, making Dahlia almost have to run to keep up with him.

"Stone, my point is that there are no guarantees—at the boarding school or on the ranch," she told him, sounding slightly out of breath.

He slowed his steps, allowing her to catch up with him.

"All we can do is try to keep Field as safe as physically possible, without wrapping him up in tissue paper and sticking him in a drawer somewhere."

Stone flinched at the accusation, remembering how he'd always hated it when his dad or Blade had worried about him or, worse, tried to stop him from doing something he wanted to do because, in their opinion, the risk was too great. Stone had never thought too much about a risk being too great—but now he did.

"The main job of a parent is to see to it a child is happy," Dahlia went on. "Or at least to avoid making him unhappy on purpose."

"Dahlia, for the last time, I'm not sending Field away to school in order to make him miserable," he said tightly. "Has it ever occurred to you that I might want more for my son than I had growing up? This school can provide that. It has stuff like music appreciation, art, literature, sports, computer skills—plus, he'll be associating with kids of different backgrounds and cultures. Ranch life can be isolating and restricting a good deal of the time. And awfully lonely.'' He ended with a sigh.

His separation from Dahlia was getting to him. The separate bedrooms, the separate lives. The distance between them appeared insurmountable, a vast wasteland of broken dreams and forgotten promises.

A marriage being slowly eaten away, a little at a time, and no way to stop it from happening.

"But he's so little..." Dahlia slid her hand into his.

Her fingers gripped his, and Stone felt the heat in his hand, then his arm, traveling a well-worn path directly to his heart—and suddenly he couldn't think.

All he could do was feel.

Dahlia looked up at him, her expression dead serious as she said, "You're not sending Field toward anything, don't you see? You're only keeping him away from what he loves best.''

But Stone wasn't really listening. All he knew at that moment was how good her hand felt in his. He concentrated on the soft, slim fingers wrapped around his callused ones.

He breathed in the scent of her perfume. It was called Sunflowers or Wildflowers or Rain—something like that, but it was light and natural and earthy.

Like Dahlia herself.

Stone looked at the woman by his side as he slowed his stride to match hers. Why couldn't things stay this way, with the two of them walking hand in hand along the highway of life? With them trailing along behind Field as he raced ahead, separate, yet part of them.

But almost before that thought—that need—could take shape, another one pushed in. Relentless. Enduring. To move forward with a life that didn't include Brooke was an erasure, even a betrayal—and Stone couldn't do it.

He held fast to the loss, the pain of losing Brooke as a poignant way of remembering her.

"Stone?" Dahlia was peering up at him in concern. "What is it?"

He shrugged. And then another thought hit him. "I have a question for you," he said slowly. "Are you going to tell Field that you're an angel?"

"I...I don't know what—"

"If you really believe you're an angel, shouldn't you prepare Field?"

She looked stunned, and for a moment he took pity on her. Only...damn it, at least he wasn't in denial about Brooke's death. Maybe he was doing a lot of things wrong, but at least he was facing up to the death of his daughter.

He wanted his wife back. He wanted things to get back to normal. And he wanted somehow to shock some sense into Dahlia.

A deep sadness settled in over him, filling in all the cracks in his heart. Because, more than anything else, he wanted Dahlia to give him another chance. But he was scared that he was too late.

Dahlia sat on the park bench, across the street from Trey's Garage and Service Station. She was thinking about what Stone had said earlier.

How was she going to prepare Field? she wondered sadly. He'd already lost his sister—could he survive losing her, as well?

She stirred restlessly on the bench, her gaze seeking out her son, who was playing on the swings. Nothing seemed fair. He was so young and defenseless, and he needed her as much as he needed Stone.

Dahlia pressed her fingers against her forehead and massaged her temples as she strained to reason her way through this dilemma. She was virtually torn between her two children—a mother's worst nightmare—and her head was beginning to throb.

She had fallen in love with Field the instant she saw him, a toddler learning to walk, a baby yearning for a woman's touch, a mother's love. His first year of life had been spent with four young men who had loved him and played with him—but the toddler had blossomed under her care.

Dahlia had encouraged him to love books and painting and gardening, as well as the more masculine pursuits— anything that caught Field's interest. She'd been his only maternal influence in a strictly male world. And she loved Field totally and completely—just as much as if he'd been her own child.

But he wasn't.

In her heart, yes. But he hadn't come from her body. Her blood didn't run through his veins. Brooke was part of her flesh, and losing her own child had been like losing the most important, the most valuable, part of herself.

Dahlia looked up when she felt Stone's presence, up, up into her husband's beautiful gray eyes, shadowed now with worry and concern.

"What's wrong?" Stone set three bottles of soda and a sack of food he was carrying on the bench, knelt in front of her and took her hands in both of his. "Are you sick? Dizzy?"

Dahlia could see the worry in Stone's troubled gaze.

"I'm okay," she said weakly, but she knew she didn't sound at all convincing. "My head hurts a little," she elaborated.

"Maybe you're just hungry."

The strong odor of chili dogs coming from the sack beside her was making her mouth water, and she nodded.

"Couldn't hurt," she said with a grin, and watched the relief enter his eyes.

Stone quickly pressed a cold bottle of soda into her hands. "You probably got too hot walking so far in the heat." He unwrapped her hot dog and waited while she took a bite of it.

And because he was watching her anxiously, Dahlia made a low sound of pleasure as she quickly devoured half her hot dog. She didn't want him worrying needlessly about her. She was fine. She was hungry and thirsty, and the food and soft drink were settling nicely in her stomach.

Stone caught Field's eye and signaled that lunch had arrived. But as they watched Field bounding toward them, Stone added, "I shouldn't have made you walk in this heat, but I was afraid to leave you out there alone with just Field. Damn," he added on a sigh. "I should have listened to Flint and got a car phone."

Dahlia laughed and nearly choked. When she could speak, she teased, "Since when did you get so progressive?"

Stone held out a hot dog and soda to Field. "What's that supposed to mean?" But a grin was forming.

"You're technically challenged."

Stone sat down beside her and opened his own lunch. "I beg your pardon? Didn't I just spend hard-earned money on a computer system for the ranch that could possibly send the sheep to another planet?"

Field laughed out loud and they both looked at him. He was sitting on the ground, looking happy and relaxed for the first time in a long time.

"Face it, Dad," he said, "Shannon knows more about computers than you do."

"We've had the computer for weeks and you haven't touched it," Dahlia added.

"But what does that have to do with a car phone?" Stone wanted to know.

Dahlia and Field looked at each other and grinned. "You don't like modern technology of any kind," Dahlia informed him. "Car phones, answering machines, video games—anything with buttons you shy away from. I'm surprised you use doorbells."

Stone held his bottle of soda over her head, tilting it just enough to make her squeal and move slightly away from him. "Are you saying I'm old-fashioned?" he asked.

"You are when it comes to a few of the more modern conveniences."

Taking a thirsty swallow of his drink, Stone frowned. "But that computer system Flint made us buy—"

"You fought just as hard against using the drive-through window when the new bank was built."

"But it almost feels like stealing when you run a little plastic card through a slit in the side of a bank and cash comes shooting out," he grumbled.

And Dahlia grinned, thinking they were actually sitting here laughing and talking as a family. Just the way they used to.

Stone was a man better suited for the 1940s or 1950s, she thought with warm affection. When life was lived at a much slower pace. When people could leave their doors unlocked at night. When you could get real ice-cream sodas at the drugstore, instead of making your own at home.

He was a good man, kind, gentle, generous to a fault, even with all those little gadgets and new devices he resisted using. He'd been brought up on love and family and hard work—and staying together, no matter what.

He'd been brought up to be the breadwinner, to take care of his family, to slay the dragons that threatened his wife or children and to slay those dragons alone.

But he hadn't been brought up to love and raise a child...and then watch her die.

Dahlia finished eating and watched the two men in her life devour a hot dog each and then share a second. Then Stone brought out a bag of cookies, and the three of them went through the treat in record time.

It was a quiet, peaceful time, warm and happy, like before—with Brooke—and Dahlia cherished it.

After lunch, Field raced off to play on the swings and Stone suggested a walk, if she was feeling up to it. Dahlia bounded to her feet and tucked her hand into his. "Are you kidding? My headache's gone. I feel stuffed with cookies," she added ruefully. "But other than that, I'm feeling on top of the world. Wanna race to the baseball field and back?"

Stone slid his arm around her instead. "Let's walk. When the doctor told me to take care of you, I don't think he meant engaging in a race across the park."

Dahlia happily agreed and they started off. Before they had taken two steps, she said, "Remember the first time we brought Field here? He was just learning to walk and he fell in love with the swings. You spent hours sitting on the swing with him in your lap, gently moving back and forth."

Stone smiled—the first real one she'd seen for a while. "He put his arms out on either side and made sputtering noises like an airplane."

"And you were convinced he was going to grow up to be a pilot." She paused, and then she said slowly, "Remember the first time we brought Brooke here? She played in the sandbox for hours that day."

Stone hesitated and then replied, "She acted like she'd never seen a sandbox before."

Dahlia laughed gently. "Stone, do you think we had boring kids?" she asked him. "One spent hours pretending she was at the beach. The other spent hours, weeks, months, pretending he was a plane.''

Stone's grin widened. ''I think we had two normal, healthy kids.''

''I remember something else.''

''What's that?'' He tugged her just a bit closer to him, and she didn't resist.

''You bought Field the biggest, most expensive swing set you could find and had it delivered the next day.''

''I remember.''

She sighed softly. It felt good to talk this way, to remember the many good times instead of the bad.

Quickly, so she wouldn't break the fragile emotional connection growing between them, she said, ''We were going to build a home of our own, an A-frame log cabin in the woods. Remember that? So we could look down at the river.''

''I remember.''

''I guess it's too late now,'' she said slowly, her heart wrenching at the sound of his soft, slow voice. Because she knew she wouldn't be staying.

Stone didn't respond immediately, but then he looked at her and said, ''Why is it too late? Now that I think of it, it's a great idea. We stopped work on the house or even talking about it because…because the timing wasn't right. But you've wanted that house for years, and so have I. Why shouldn't we build it?'' He paused. ''It might be the best thing for us to do.''

Dahlia felt a deep, penetrating sadness settle around her heart as she listened to the sudden eagerness in his voice. She shouldn't have brought it up, but she'd had no idea Stone would suggest building it now! They hadn't even talked about the house since last year.

But, of course, they hadn't talked about much of anything since Brooke had died.

"We can contact the architect this afternoon, set up an appointment. The blueprints had already been completed when—" Stone broke off when she wandered away from him and stood with her fingers pressed against her temples.

When Brooke was killed.

The unfinished sentence stretched endlessly between them.

Then he walked toward her. "Why can't we build the house now?"

"It…it's just that…things could change and—"

Stone gently took her hand in both of his, his gray eyes suddenly bleak. "Come on. They're probably back with the truck by now. You need to get out of this heat."

Dahlia didn't protest. Because how could she explain that it wasn't the heat that was bothering her—it was a bewildering mixture of conflicting feelings.

She wanted to succeed with her mission and get back to Brooke. That was what she wanted. That was all she'd wanted for months. And she was running out of time. It had already been two whole weeks since she'd regained consciousness in the hospital, and so far her mission had been stalled at every turn.

She had exactly one week left.

But she hadn't expected this tidal wave of nerves, this overwhelming sadness, this…this horrifying sense of loss when she thought about leaving Stone and Field behind.

A tear rolled down her cheek, and Dahlia quickly brushed it away, hoping Stone hadn't seen it.

Stone drove toward the ranch in the rain, both hands gripping the steering wheel. Okay, so he'd accomplished what he'd wanted to do today. Field was registered in school in San Antonio, so why wasn't he feeling happy about it? Or, at least, relieved it was done?

He stared at the wet, slippery road stretched out in front of him, but all he could see was the look on Field's face as Stone signed the necessary papers to get him enrolled for the fall term. The resignation and utter defeat in his son's eyes had been worse than any display of temper.

So was the silence coming from the back seat of the car.

Was this day ever going to end? he wondered. He felt as though he'd fought a war today—and lost.

And maybe he had. Things were never going to be the same between him and Field, that was for damn sure. And Dahlia... His family was slipping farther and farther away from him, and he didn't know how to stop it.

For an instant today, he had felt hope rising within him. When Dahlia had mentioned the house they'd been planning to build, he had thought that maybe, just maybe, she was considering a move forward. And he had been willing to meet her halfway.

Hell, more than halfway.

Because the house was something he could give to her. Freely. Unconditionally. And without hesitation. And maybe, with a little luck, they could build a new life together along with their dream house.

Once, not too long ago, Dahlia had believed in him and their love. She'd believed in always and forever and that nothing could touch them. That was why she'd always wanted a log home in the woods, high up on the hill, near the sunshine and the stars, so nothing bad could happen to them.

That was why he'd felt so much better when she'd mentioned the house. To him, it had been a step in the right direction, a positive sign.

But he had to get Dahlia to stop believing she was an

angel. Magical thinking, the doctors at the hospital had called it. Believing in something so desperately that the person soon thinks it's true. They kept saying she had to face up to Brooke's death before she could do anything else. Stone had to prove to Dahlia that she was made of flesh and blood, and had a heart and soul.

But how? How could he do that without alienating her completely?

An idea took hold and slowly started to take shape.

Chapter Five

Stone stood on the front porch and breathed in the warm night air, heavy and damp. It was eerily quiet out here, he noticed, as though the entire ranch was holding its breath.

Watching and waiting.

But for what?

For Dahlia to come to grips with the reality of Brooke's death? For her to divorce him and walk away? Or, more than likely, waiting for him to pick up the pieces of his life and go forward as a husband and father, regardless of the pain and grief he felt?

One thing was for sure, Stone thought, looking out across the ranch. Something had to be done, something had to change—and soon. Because none of them could go on much longer, living in the same house, yet separate, lost and alone.

Field had been holed up in the barn since they'd arrived home that afternoon, refusing to speak a word to anyone— even to Rocky. And Dahlia was locked up in Brooke's room, silent and alone, but that accusing silence spoke volumes.

The screen door opened and his younger brother appeared. Stone heard the garbled sound of a news bulletin interrupting regular programming as it repeated its important message.

"Thought you'd like to know the hurricane's definitely headed this way," Rocky told him. "Should be here, full tilt, in less than forty-eight hours."

Stone nodded. The wind was already picking up. And it was just what they needed—a hurricane. Perfect timing. Like tempers around here weren't short enough as it was.

Stone knew exactly what he had to do. He'd known for weeks. But he also knew he didn't stand a glacier's chance in hell.

But he had to try.

He had to pick up the pieces of his life—and Dahlia's, too—and he had to do it now. Tonight.

His life had broken apart one year ago, large pieces of it crushed beyond recognition. Even so, one piece, shining and pure, yet sharp enough to draw blood, a piece Stone could hold on to, was solid and it was real.

He was still deeply, hopelessly in love with Dahlia—and he'd do anything, absolutely anything, not to lose her.

Anything.

Even if it meant he had to risk his heart all over again.

Stone took a deep, ragged breath, not knowing if he could do it or not, but he had to try. Because all he knew for certain was what he must do. It was as clear as a finger pointing out the only path he must take to redeem himself in Dahlia's eyes.

Dahlia was brushing her hair when she heard the knock on Brooke's bedroom door. She let Stone in, then stood back, waiting.

"You win," he stated softly.

Dahlia looked up at him. There was something else in his steady gaze, something that startled her to the very core. It was the light shining from his gray eyes, like a beam cast by a lighthouse over stormy seas, leading the way home.

"What do you mean I've won?" she asked him slowly.

"Field doesn't have to go to boarding school."

Dahlia sucked in her breath—hard. She couldn't believe her stubborn, hardheaded husband was willing to listen to reason. What could he possibly be up to now?

"That's nice," she said warily.

"You don't believe me." He closed the door behind him and leaned casually against it.

To block her exit from the room if she didn't go along with whatever he was planning next? Dahlia quickly shook off that less-than-angelic thought and wondered how on earth she'd become so suspicious.

And of her own husband, too.

"I believe you," she said quietly. "But...but why? What made you change your mind?"

Stone placed gentle hands on her shoulders. "My mind's not set in concrete, regardless of what you might think." But he didn't sound irritable or impatient. Just...resigned.

"Only a few hours ago—"

"I was wrong, okay?" Now he sounded mildly irritated. "I forget sometimes how little Field is—"

"But you've been saying all along that he was old enough to live in a boarding school," she protested. She was aware of the warmth of his fingers as they slid down her arms to grip her hands.

"Dahlia." His sigh was weary. "Why are you arguing with me?"

"I'm not! I'm just trying to understand your reasons."

"Field needs us more than I thought," he said quietly.

Us. That one word felt as though a dagger had been plunged into her heart.

Oh dear, why was she arguing with him? Stone was doing what she wanted. Why didn't she just leave it alone and gracefully accept what he was giving her?

Instead she said, "You've already given the school a deposit."

Stone shrugged. "We'll get it back."

Dahlia didn't care about the money, but she latched on to it anyway, stalling for time. "And if you don't? That's an awful lot of money just to throw away...."

She became aware of the way Stone was looking at her. Puzzled was not quite the word to describe the expression in his eyes. But it was close. Maybe absolute, total bewilderment was a far better description.

She pulled her hands out of his and wandered over to stand at the windows of Brooke's bedroom. It had started to rain again. Even as she stood and watched, the raindrops became bigger, rounder and slashed against the windowpanes.

At that moment she truly wanted to run into Stone's arms and stay there, just as she'd done so many times in the past. But coming home to Stone meant leaving Brooke behind.

And if she did that, she'd never see her beautiful little daughter again.

Dahlia pressed her fingertips against the cold glass of the windowpane, desperately wanting to feel something, anything, other than the pain of being ripped in two.

He'd said Field could stay on the ranch.

Dahlia suddenly felt as though she'd been dumped into

deep water without knowing how to swim. Stone and Field would be together, a family, which was exactly what she wanted for the two of them.

"I've been thinking of something else tonight." Stone was now standing behind her, not touching her, but she could still feel the warmth of him.

And sense his need for her.

Dahlia held her breath, waiting. She didn't want him trying to get her into bed again.

Not again.

And not tonight.

Because tonight she just wasn't strong enough to resist.

"I've been thinking that I was wrong not to consider your feelings. And what you need."

Dahlia was surprised by the statement. And by the unexpected, touchingly vulnerable note that had crept into Stone's low voice. She turned slowly to face him.

Stone took her in his arms and held her gently, as though she might break at any moment. And Dahlia allowed him to hold her. It wouldn't hurt anything, would it? To seek comfort in her husband's arms? Or would it somehow keep Basil from coming for her?

"I'm not sure what you're saying," she said hesitantly.

"You've wanted another baby for months now. A baby we'd already agreed upon. A baby we both wanted." Stone's voice remained low and gentle as he kissed her cheek and then her earlobe.

Dahlia grew cold inside, and her hands started to tremble. "That was before. I was wrong to think I could replace Brooke with another child." The cold fear was rapidly turning into heat as Stone pulled her more snugly against him.

"You weren't doing that." Her kissed her and Dahlia responded without thinking. "You wanted to focus on the positive things in life. You wanted to move forward and I…didn't,'' he said softly.

"What are you trying to tell me?"

He took a deep, hard breath. ''That we should have another baby.''

Dahlia stared up at him, unable to speak. She was in shock.

Stone wanted another baby? Just like that—he wanted another baby? Profound joy ripped through her. He was offering her a life without Brooke, and Dahlia knew what that must be costing him emotionally.

But how could she accept his wonderful gift?

How could she?

To accept a life without Brooke meant never touching or holding her daughter again!

And if she turned away, if she tossed aside Stone's precious gift and found her way back to Brooke, then what would that do to him?

And what would it do to Field? Her heart cried out in protest, torn between Brooke on one side and Stone, Field and a new baby to love on the other.

Misery tumbled through her. She didn't know what to do now! She didn't know what to do!

After the longest time, Stone spoke again. ''What's wrong?'' He frowned uncertainly. ''That's what you want, isn't it? Another child? Just like we planned?''

It used to be what she wanted—but not now. Oh God help her, not now! It was too late. It was much too late! Dahlia felt the tears beginning deep inside her.

She swallowed hard, several times, unable to catch her breath. Stone wanted the two of them to have another baby? Now? After all those months of begging him to reconsider?

Begging him to at least talk to her about it. About what

he felt and what he thought. And why the idea of having another baby had been so frightening to him.

He'd been so dead set against it. And he'd refused to talk to her. To acknowledge her feelings. And that hadn't been like Stone at all. Not the Stone she'd married.

But Dahlia remembered the brutal pain in his eyes whenever she brought up the subject.

So she'd stopped bringing it up.

As though he'd read her mind, Stone rushed in, his voice quiet, but insistent. "I should have listened to you months ago, and I'm sorry. I was wrong not to listen to you. But I wasn't against having another child because I didn't want more children. I just didn't want to lose anyone else."

He didn't want to lose anyone else? Was that why he was offering her another child—to pacify her? Giving in to her because he didn't want to be left alone, as his ex-wife had left him alone years ago?

And even if he meant every word he was saying, Dahlia realized a new baby couldn't solve what was wrong between the two of them. Having another child couldn't solve this complete lack of faith in Stone's heart.

And Dahlia wasn't about to have another child, only to raise him or her in a glass cage.

"Dahlia, are you listening to me?" Stone asked when she turned away. "Things will get better between us. You'll see. I know I've been shutting you out, making all these decisions without you, not talking to you about what I was feeling."

It sounded as though Stone meant what he was saying. And she was beginning to believe his offer wasn't some trick to snap her out of believing she was an angel. Any other time and Dahlia would be overjoyed at the way he was finally opening up to her.

And normally she would have been filled with hope for them—and their marriage.

But it was too late. And now she had to get back to heaven! Back to her daughter, Brooke!

Dahlia wandered over to the handmade wooden rocking horse they'd given Brooke for her fourth birthday. She'd wanted a real horse that year, too. And every Christmas and birthday after that. A real, live, breathing horse of her own. That was all she'd ever wanted.

"You were right about something else, too," he said. "Field's had enough disruption in his life. He does need to stay here with us. I realized that today."

Stone's voice sounded far off and she couldn't concentrate on what he was saying.

He was actually considering—no, suggesting—that they have another baby? Another daughter, perhaps? Or a son? Field would like that, Dahlia knew. A baby brother for him to protect.

She ran her fingertips tenderly over the smooth, polished surface of the rocking horse, over its head and down its mane. The thought of having another baby, of Stone actually agreeing to it, was more than she could comprehend right now.

"And, if you still want to, we can build that house in the woods, just like I promised when we first got married," he said.

Their house in the woods.

For nine years they'd lived with his brothers in the family homestead, saving every cent they could in order to build a home of their own. It wasn't that the house wasn't large enough for all of them, or that Blade and Rocky didn't respect their privacy. But the Victorian house belonged to the Tyler men. It didn't belong to her.

Dahlia had always dreamed of having a home of her

own. Ever since she was a small child, often uprooted from some temporary housing on an Air Force base, she had longed for a house with her name on the deed, to furnish and decorate. And Stone had understood that need.

They'd spent many nights through the years planning their home, pouring part of themselves into every little detail. From their loft bedroom with huge skylight, so they could sleep under the stars, to the fieldstone fireplace in the living room. It had been a family affair, too, with Field and Brooke throwing in their suggestions.

But after Brooke was killed, Stone had lost interest in the house.

He'd lost interest in life.

And now he'd regained that interest. He was willing to try—but what on earth was she supposed to do now? Why couldn't Stone have talked to her like this nine months ago? Or six months ago?

Or even last month?

But it was too late for them to be a family now. Fate had intervened and sent her to Basil and the gates of heaven.

"Dahlia?" Stone said, interrupting her thoughts. "Did you hear me? It's going to be okay now, sweetheart. I swear."

She nodded dumbly, but didn't turn around. Why was this happening? She had succeeded in her mission, hadn't she? Stone was letting Field remain on the ranch.

Then what was taking Basil so long?

Stone and Field would be okay now, she thought. She was sure of it. Tonight, Stone had proven that he was still the reasonable, levelheaded and tenderhearted man she'd married. Now that he was finally ready to face his future, his life would be one of joy and happiness.

But she hadn't planned on being included!

"Do you want to go out to the barn with me and tell Field the good news?" Once again he was standing behind her.

Dahlia nodded. She accepted the hand he extended toward her, and walked with him out of Brooke's bedroom and down the back stairs.

But inside, a thousand conflicting thoughts and feelings tumbled around, bumping into each other with increasing speed. She was feeling and thinking about far too much to understand any of it right now.

Only one thing was crystal clear—this whole mission was becoming far too complicated!

They dashed into the barn, bringing the wind and the rain with them. Stone watched Dahlia shove back the hood on her multicolored raincoat and shake out her hair, thinking how disarmingly beautiful she was, even in foul weather.

But he fondly remembered walking in the rain with her along the streets of San Antonio before they were married. And the way she'd sing "Raindrops Keep Falling on My Head," totally unaware of the amused looks from others on the street. She knew she had a terrible singing voice, but she didn't care.

Another memory drifted through his mind. Dahlia, holding Brooke and singing her softly to sleep when their daughter was an infant. Stone willed himself to think of something else to block the pain, but he couldn't get that beautiful moment out of his head.

And then he didn't want to. He allowed the memory to play itself out, with all its bittersweet pain, and afterward he felt better. And he felt as though he'd taken a major step forward tonight.

He followed Dahlia toward the far corner of the barn,

where his son was sitting on the ground, watching the sleeping puppies. Ginger was nestled down between them, keeping a wary eye on Field, but Stone noticed the herding dog didn't look too worried.

He'd expected Dahlia to rush over and announce the news that Field would be staying on the ranch with them. But to his surprise, she merely sat down on the ground next to Field and asked, "Which one do you like the best?"

"That one." Field promptly pointed out the collie pup who was nearest him.

Dahlia leaned over to let Ginger sniff her hand and lick her fingers before she carefully petted the rust-and-cream-colored puppy. "She's a good choice for a pet. Don't you agree, Stone?" She looked up at him expectantly.

Stone gazed back at her, trying not to grin. "Sure, why not?" he said, watching Field look quickly at one and then the other of his parents.

"Whose pet?" he asked suspiciously, gray eyes wary.

"Yours, of course." Dahlia ruffled his dark head affectionately. "Your dad and I have been talking, and we've decided that it's time you accepted more responsibility on the ranch. Like taking full responsibility for raising this little one here. You think you can do that?"

Field stared at her blankly. "You mean on weekends." His voice was somewhere between flat resignation of his boarding school fate and excitement over having a puppy of his own.

Dahlia looked up at Stone.

Stone squatted down in front of his son. "No, all the time. In five or six weeks, after the puppy's weaned, we'll put a wire cage in your room until she's housebroken—" Stone broke off as Field launched himself into his arms.

It was a hard, forgiving hug, then Field was pulling away, his gaze darting to meet his mother's, then slowly returning to Stone's. "You're not sending me away?" he asked hopefully.

"Not until we pack you off for college." Stone struggled to keep his voice light. The stark relief in his son's eyes was painful to watch.

"Is...is Mom staying, too?"

Stone grew still. "Of course she is, Field," he said softly. "Why would you ask something like that?"

"Because you're always fighting with her. And... and..."

Dahlia took Field's hand gently in hers. "And what, sweetie?" she prompted, when it looked as though Field had no idea how to finish his sentence.

"Last year when Matthew's dad started fighting with his mom, she left. They got a divorce."

Dahlia's blue gaze quickly met Stone's as she said, "We're not getting a divorce."

"Promise?"

Stone cleared his throat. "Everything's going to be okay, Field." He was going to see to it personally.

"You won't fight with Mom again, will you?" The question burst out of him, and before Stone could reply, Field added with sudden, low fury, "I hate it when you fight with her! I hate it!"

"Okay." Stone hauled him close. Field was holding on to him as though he never intended to let go ever again. Stone could actually feel the child's terror.

Dear Lord, what had they done to him this past year? he thought, still stunned by his son's outburst. First the deadening silence after Brooke's accident, then the endless tension that would suddenly erupt into shouting matches.

And then Stone had wanted to send his only son away from him, away from all the people who loved him—and for what?

He tightened his grip on Field as he wondered if he'd been insane since Brooke's death. Because to him, it sure as hell looked like it.

"Field, listen to me." Stone spoke to the small face burrowing into his left shoulder. "Fighting with someone doesn't mean you don't love them or want to be with them."

Dahlia had dropped to her knees beside them and was now stroking Field's hair with gentle fingers. Her rose-scented perfume drifted over Stone, her hair brushing against his hand as she bent to kiss their son's wet cheek.

Stone had to swallow hard before continuing. "Fighting isn't always a bad thing. Sometimes people need to yell to be heard." His gaze locked on Dahlia's and his voice softened even more. "It doesn't mean you've stopped loving them."

Dahlia's eyes never left his face as she added, "Your dad's right, sweetie. Adults do fight sometimes, just like kids do. It's nothing to be afraid of."

At the sound of her voice, Field raised his head and looked at her. "Are you sure?" he asked hopefully.

"I'm sure." Dahlia kissed him again and paused to brush away fresh tears that had escaped down his little cheek. "What are you going to name your puppy?" she asked.

Field rubbed at his eyes fiercely and then shifted around to look at his little charge. "I don't know." He turned away as he thoughtfully considered the matter.

"You do realize, don't you," Stone said to Dahlia in a low voice, "that you just gave our son an expensive, pure-bred herding dog for a pet. I don't want to hear what Blade will have to say about this."

"Oh, he'll grumble and complain some, and then come home with a wicker basket for the puppy to sleep in," she said cheerfully.

Stone laughed. "Yeah, with a big, thick cushion so the puppy can be comfortable."

"Hey, I got it!" Field turned toward them excitedly. "Tiger!"

"But she's a girl," Dahlia protested.

Stone watched as Field thought about it. Then he said, "What about Tiger Rose?"

Dahlia laughed. "Tiger Rose, it is. A perfect name for a perfect little puppy."

Stone was relieved—and truly amazed—at how fast a kid could switch emotional gears. His gaze wandered over to Dahlia. It was too bad adults couldn't do the same.

Dahlia sat there quietly, watching every move they made, listening to every word they said—as though etching this moment into her memory.

For some point in the near future when she would no longer be with either of them?

Stone had no idea why the thought had even entered his head. He knew what he'd done tonight wouldn't solve all their problems, but at least it was a start.

"Dad?"

Stone ruffled his son's dark hair. "Yeah?"

"Everything okay now?"

He smiled. "Everything's okay."

But then Stone noticed an expression in Dahlia's blue eyes that could only be described as sad. And suddenly he wasn't all that certain he'd told Field the truth.

Chapter Six

Later that night Dahlia carefully smoothed the pale pink lotion all over her body, before applying the light dusting of rose-scented powder. Brooke had given her a complete set for Mother's Day, and for months after the accident, Dahlia couldn't bear to look at it.

But now she used it faithfully every night after her bath. She felt close to her daughter each time she caught a whiff of the delicate fragrance.

After putting on her thigh-length white sleep shirt, she glanced out the window as the rain slashed against the glass. It had stopped pouring for the moment, but the wind pounded the house, making it hard for her to relax.

Her gaze skidded longingly about the room. The pink-and-white-striped wallpaper was so pretty with the pale pink trim and woodwork. Decorating this room when Brooke was four had been the happiest time in Dahlia's life. They had spent weeks planning to turn the room from a nursery into a bedroom for a "big girl."

Dahlia paced, forgetting to put on her robe or slippers,

forgetting everything but the little girl she'd loved so un-conditionally. The house was quiet, everyone else was sound asleep by now. But she'd grown to love this time of night, with no one around to keep her from indulging in memories of Brooke.

But tonight there was no sense of the peace she usually felt. Dahlia was on edge as she waited. Had Basil forgotten about her?

She took Brooke's Cabbage Patch doll off the shelf and cradled it in her arms as she walked back and forth. What was Basil waiting for? she wondered uncertainly. She'd done what he'd asked, hadn't she? She'd made Stone be-lieve in the future again. What was Basil up to?

Dahlia sighed regretfully, hating the idea that she wouldn't be included in Stone's lavish plans for their fu-ture.

A new home.

A new baby.

And a new life—without Brooke in it.

She couldn't stand still. She replaced the doll on the shelf and wandered around the room, allowing her fingers to slide over various items that her daughter had loved.

A huge stuffed rabbit that had been a gift from Rocky her first Easter. A copy of *Little Women* that had once be-longed to Dahlia. Brooke had kept it on her night table until she was old enough for Dahlia to read it to her. And, of course, her teddy bear collection.

She circled the room once more, trying to concentrate on Brooke—and block out her regrets toward Field.

And Stone.

They'd be okay, she told herself over and over again. They had each other, and the rest of the Tyler family. Blade and Flint and Rocky would be there for Stone. His brothers would help him raise Field.

Come on, Basil! She was impatient and felt disgustingly healthy. Let's just do it. What are you waiting for? A gust of wind rattled the windows, making her jump.

The hurricane would be here within forty-eight hours, Rocky had said. This time of year was normally hurricane season, so she tried to dismiss her anxiety. But it wasn't easy. She was filled with questions and this weather wasn't making things any easier.

Dahlia turned to stare out the windows and watched the trees in the distance, swaying in the heavy winds. And she thought back to the picnic by the stream, the day Field had found his lump of gold at the end of the rainbow. Stone had wanted proof she was an angel that day....

Her heart started pounding. Could it be...? Was it possible that...that Basil had sent the hurricane as a sign of things to come?

Oh, she hoped so. Because she wanted this to be over soon. She wanted it over with before—

Before what? Before she changed her mind? Was that it? Was that what she was trying so desperately to ignore? The questions tumbled around inside her head, and for the first time since she'd awakened in the hospital, Dahlia felt unsettled. Uncertain that giving up Stone and Field for Brooke was the right thing to do.

She spun around and quickly paced in the opposite direction as though to run away from her deepest wishes. If she changed her mind and stayed, then she couldn't see Brooke again. It was that simple.

And she had to see her daughter again. Be with her again. She just had to! Brooke was her baby, her own flesh and blood! What was so terrible about wanting to be with her own daughter?

Because it means leaving Stone and Field behind, a voice

in her head stated flatly. The clear voice of reason. And love.

Unable to stay in Brooke's room a moment longer, Dahlia yanked open the door to the bathroom, which was nestled between the children's two bedrooms. Field was undoubtedly asleep, but she quietly peeked in.

The nightlight in the bathroom illuminated his room, which was such an expression of the little boy's vivid personality that Dahlia smiled. Navy blue and fire-engine red were the primary colors. The clear, energetic colors were in an array of solids, stripes and plaids, giving relief to the stark, empty white walls.

The shelves were neatly crammed with books and puzzles and games. There was nothing fussy about this room—or about Field. He was open, honest and direct. Quick to take offense, quick to forgive. A truly loving, impulsive child.

He had kicked his covers off, and Dahlia slipped in to tuck the thick, navy blue comforter around his shoulders. She bent to kiss his cheek and then straightened. She had the sudden, almost overwhelming desire to make certain Stone would take good care of his son.

Dahlia crossed the room and opened the door to the hall, filled with uneasiness. What if Stone had only been humoring her? What if Basil knew he hadn't really meant it when he'd said Field could stay here? Maybe that was why she wasn't back at the gate by now.

Worse, what if Stone planned to let Field stay home for now, earning his son's trust, and then sent him away at a later date? What would that do to their relationship?

It would destroy it.

Dahlia closed the door to Field's room and glanced at the door directly across the hall. There was a light on under

Stone's door. Good, he was still up. She took a deep breath and tapped lightly.

The door swung open and her breath caught in her throat. It was all she could do to steady the tide of emotion crashing through her. Stone was wearing jeans, a thick white T-shirt and he was barefoot. His long, dark hair was damp from a recent shower, and he smelled like soap and freshly washed cotton.

He'd been reading instead of sleeping, Dahlia noticed as he stepped back to let her into the room. The enormous bed with its tall, hand-carved headboard was still made, the peach and green comforter neatly in place, making Dahlia flash back to when the bed had been a tangle of covers with the two of them locked in each other's arms. Night after night and lots of mornings, as well.

But that seemed like a lifetime ago.

A book was facedown on a rocker, a denim shirt tossed over the back. A cup of what looked to be coffee was on the table with the lamp. The table that nestled between the two matching rocking chairs in the bay window area of the room.

Only her rocking chair hadn't been used in months. Not since she'd moved into Brooke's room, because she'd been unable to stand the silence and the loneliness in this one.

She turned quickly to face him. "I didn't mean to disturb you."

"You're not disturbing me," he broke in softly.

Dahlia watched as his gaze skidded briefly over her bare arms and legs, and the sudden hot look in his eyes made her wish she'd remembered to put on her robe.

"I'll only stay a minute—"

"You can stay the whole night."

She stared up at his face, deeply carved by the sun and the wind and a thousand worries over the years. Especially this last one. And she had this huge, fierce, physical longing to reach up and touch him, to bury her fingers in his dark hair.

She'd left his bedroom last spring, mostly because she couldn't bear to be near him when he kept shutting her out of his life, when he wouldn't allow her to mention Brooke's name in his presence, when he steadfastly refused to talk about his own pain.

And the way he kept ignoring her wish for another baby. Another daughter, another son—it hadn't mattered. Just another baby to love and raise to adulthood.

That seemed, at the time, the only way to get past what had happened to Brooke. To have faith that another child, born of their love for each other, would somehow survive to grow up.

Only now...Dahlia had no idea how Stone felt toward her, despite what he'd said about wanting to have another baby. And she found his casual statement about staying the whole night with him to be unintentionally cruel.

Dahlia sat down in her rocking chair and folded her hands primly in her lap. "I'd like to talk to you, if I may."

"Sure." He perched on the antique trunk at the foot of the bed and waited for her to begin.

Dahlia, feeling his gaze as it raked over her, wished desperately for a robe or something to cover herself. She shivered.

"Are you cold?"

"A little," she lied. She wasn't cold. She felt much too warm to be feeling cold. Before he could respond to her complaint, Dahlia grabbed the denim shirt he'd left on his rocking chair and put it on.

Which was a big mistake. Because it was the shirt he'd had on earlier that evening. The faint scent of him that lingered sent fresh waves of doubt thundering through her.

Was she wrong to leave him? To completely ignore what they'd once had together?

But she'd tried so hard to reach him, tried for months— until she'd been drained of all hope.

And now it was too late.

Dahlia wrapped herself in Stone's shirt and sat down again, rolling the sleeves up enough for her hands to be free. She tried to stem the doubts rushing through her, but had little success.

"What would you like to talk about?" Stone asked patiently.

"About Field."

He waited, but Dahlia didn't know how to continue. She was distracted, startled into an awareness of how handsome her husband looked these days. Constant exposure to the outdoors had left him with a deep tan, and his hair, as dark as the night, was much longer than usual, as though he couldn't be bothered to get it cut.

And his eyes…they were the color of the river at dusk, soft, mellow, like liquid silver.…

Her gaze wandered uneasily over the length of his deceptively relaxed frame, and she suddenly felt tiny bubble bursts of excitement, attraction, confusion—all rolled into one heart-throbbing emotion.

Dahlia's thoughts went wandering suddenly into erotic directions they hadn't traveled in since Brooke had died, which surprised her.

"What about Field?" Stone prodded gently.

Her thoughts skidded back to reality. "I need to know if Field's going to be all right."

Stone looked at her closely. "Why wouldn't he be?"

"I don't know." She shifted restlessly in the chair, as she tried to push away the physical awareness that he'd aroused in her. She hadn't been this aware of Stone, this tuned in to him as a man, for months—except, of course, the night of their moonlight dance in the rose garden.

But why was this happening now? Why was she feeling so sexually awakened, a purely human trait, when she should be feeling, er, more spiritual and angelic?

She didn't understand what was happening to her, why she felt so confused. She had to stay focused because she was running out of time. She had to restore Stone's faith in himself, and she only had a few days left.

"I…I guess I'm afraid you'll change your mind. About sending him away to school," Dahlia added, when he didn't respond to her concern. "Please, promise me you won't do that."

Stone slid off the heavy trunk and knelt before her chair. "Field's not going anywhere," he stated softly, unclenching her balled-up fists and holding her hands in his. "Not until he starts college—like I said earlier."

Dahlia breathed a big sigh of relief and smiled at her husband. He was more like himself tonight than he'd been the entire past year. And when he smiled back at her—a warm, direct, uncomplicated smile that made her breath catch slightly—she knew she was in big, big trouble.

She'd always been drawn to long-legged six-footers for some reason. Add the sweet and sexy grin that came slow and easy, and the heat that was steadily growing in Stone's eyes—and she was hooked.

It was just as it had been on the day she met him, nine years earlier. Blindsided by a divorced sheep rancher with a toddler to raise. Three things she'd sworn to avoid, because, at twenty-one, she hadn't needed the hassle. But she'd never regretted her decision to marry him. Not once.

Stone leaned forward and kissed her tentatively. Dahlia held perfectly still, imagining that if she made the slightest movement, she'd shatter. Like very old, fine china.

When she didn't push him away—when, in fact, she kissed him back—Stone pulled her into his arms. Dahlia slid off the chair, her bare knees sinking into the rug, her arms wrapping tightly around him as he kissed her warmly, deeply, thoroughly.

Kissing Stone was like walking through a minefield, she thought as all five of her senses reeled. Any moment now, she expected the bomb to go off and blow her to pieces. It was him—the promise, the threat, the absolute certainty of mind-blowing passion.

Passion that had grown and blossomed into a shared history, a deeper understanding, an intuitive give-and-take, of love and heat and need and mutual respect. Through good times…and bad.

Dahlia let the memories and the look and feel of Stone fill her mind and heart and soul. And for a few crazy, sweet moments she was totally lost, and didn't notice, or care, when he guided her down to the soft, sea green rug, as each kiss blended hungrily into the next.

He'd turned to her fully now, and no living, breathing, red-blooded woman could be unaware of his intentions. Dahlia felt suspended, caught between two magnetic points—each pulling at her, tearing her apart, wanting to stay forever in his arms.…

And wanting to go to Brooke.

She suddenly found herself wanting both with equal ferocity.

She'd wanted to make love this past year, a dozen times or more, but only to create a baby. She'd never wanted to make love for herself. Or for Stone.

Tonight was different. It wasn't about making a baby. It was about building a relationship, a new life.

It was about building a future, and she knew all too painfully that it was too late for that!

She wanted him, but she had to stop him and stop him now. Dahlia felt the panic coming in waves, crushing her, making her head hurt and suddenly she couldn't breathe.

She wrenched herself out of his arms.

Shock stunned him for an instant. The sudden absence of warmth and soft, passionate response was more than Stone could take in. But then he saw Dahlia, pale and stricken, her face buried in her hands, and he edged closer.

"What's wrong? Are you sick?"

She mumbled something into her hands and shook her head. A long, shuddering, heartfelt sigh escaped.

"I didn't hear you." He gently brushed a lock of blond hair behind her left ear, fingers lingering on her cheek, fingers that shook with pent-up desire. He loved the feel of her. He always had.

"I can't," she said through her hands.

A splinter of glass, sharp and pure, wedged itself into his heart and started to grow with each additional word that came out of her mouth.

"I...I can't do this—"

"What? What can't you do?" He kept his voice deliberately low and even, trying to stem his frustration. "You can't feel or hope or...or respond to me?"

She shook her head.

"Which one can't you do?" The glass splinter in his heart was now the size and shape of a candle taper, wedging in deeply, threatening to split his heart in two.

"All of them. It...it's too late, Stone, don't you see?"

Stone took a deep, ragged breath, reached out and dragged her hands away from her face until she was forced to look at him. "Why is it too late?" he asked, his voice gentle.

She shook her head vehemently.

"And yet you feel a lot of things, don't you? You still

think and worry about Field. And me," he added softly. "You respond to both of us."

"I'm an angel," she said stubbornly, looking solidly at him. "*Why* can't you believe what I'm telling you is the truth?"

Stone took a deep, ragged breath, his fingers gripping hers hard. "There are no such things as angels."

"But how do you know that? How do you know there aren't guardian angels in our lives each and every day, protecting us, and guiding us?"

"Because if there were angels watching over us, then why didn't one of them save Brooke?" he ground out. He was hurting now, too much to care what he said or how he said it.

"Angels can't interfere," she told him haltingly. "We can only guide humans, show them the way, prod them to do the right thing."

"The same way you guided me into a decision not to send Field to boarding school?" He said it flatly, softly, and groaned inwardly when she nodded.

"Exactly. You see, all you needed was a push in the right direction—"

"How do you know I'm not the angel, instead of you?" Stone asked her pointedly, slowly getting up and going to the window. He needed some distance between them. He was caught somewhere between sexual desire and gut-wrenching frustration at her refusal to rely on *him*, on their here and now, rather than fantasy. He stared outside. It had started to rain again. "What makes your ideas and opinions more important than mine?" he asked.

"They're…they're not." She sounded adamant.

"If you ask me, this angel stuff is just an excuse to get your own way," he stated flatly, hoping to get her mad or something. Anything was better—and much healthier—than what she was doing.

"My own way?"

Stone turned to face her and nearly grinned at the flash of sheer outrage in her blue eyes. "Yeah," he drawled, mostly to irritate her. "Your free will against mine—only your wishes are backed by the chief angel himself, so how can I ever hope to fight that?"

Dahlia looked confused. And Stone watched the struggle going on inside her, as she tried to decide whether to take the higher road as an angel—or not.

And because he knew which buttons to push, he said, "You wanted Field to stay on the ranch, so he's staying. You should be pleased."

Dahlia frowned uncertainly. "Then you didn't mean what you said?"

"I meant it." He grinned slowly. "But it was my own decision, a human decision, not one sent down from heaven above."

"Don't mock me!"

"I'm not mocking you." Well, he was, but not to hurt her. He peeked out the window again. The rain was getting worse. "Do you honestly believe your angelic powers had a hand in guiding me toward building our new house? Or—" he paused deliberately "—agreeing to another baby?"

Her absolute silence drew his gaze away from the rain. And what he saw made him feel as if he'd punched a hole in something precious and fragile. Anxiety began to show itself in Dahlia's eyes, sparking out in all directions, the panic so sharp, so real, he could only stand and let it slice at him.

Stone wanted desperately to take her in his arms again, to stop the verbal jousting and relive the magic they'd found earlier, but he couldn't. Fear and frustration kept him rooted to the floor. What could he possibly say to her now? he wondered. What could he do?

He'd wanted to make her fighting mad—not alienate her completely.

He started to apologize for baiting her, but the rather lost expression in her blue eyes stilled his words. Everything about her used to shout passionate energy, and he'd glimpsed that part of her earlier, for just a few minutes, but it *had* been there.

And he savored the memory, feeling an exquisite kind of joy that, for a brief time, had drowned out his own confusion and pain, the loneliness and wondering. Stone hoped like hell he could sort through this mess and find the love they'd once had.

But he couldn't do it alone.

And he didn't know what else he could do.

The pain and grief of Brooke's death was forever spilling out over all of them, and he knew no way to stop the flow. Or, at least, keep his family from drowning in it.

"Dahlia, I'm sorry," he said truthfully. "The only point I was trying to make was that—"

"That no angels exist." Dahlia sat on the rug, staring down as she traced the outline of one peach-colored tulip with her fingertip.

The thread of sadness in her voice caused the glass wedge in his heart to explode painfully, and Stone went to her. He sat down beside her, not touching her. "You want to know what really attracted me to you in the beginning?"

Dahlia glanced up, bewildered by the sudden change in topic. She shook her head.

"It was the way you believed, wholeheartedly, in living life to the fullest. You never wasted a second on things you couldn't help." He looked down at her hand on the rug between them, still idly tracing the outline of the tulip.

He hesitated and then placed his hand over hers, his fingers gripping hers gently. Stone was afraid she'd pull away, when all he wanted was to touch her, even for an instant. Because she was slipping away from him, and he felt helpless to hold on to her.

He was relieved when she didn't pull away from him.

"I had to hustle to keep up with you," he said quietly. "I think I had about three dates to get rid of all my emotional baggage from my first marriage, or I knew you wouldn't stick around."

Her smile was faint. "I would have stuck. I did stick," she said softly. "We used to stay up into the wee hours of the morning, talking those issues out."

Stone squeezed her hand. "That's what I mean—you commit to things in this fierce, protective way that I've always admired."

"You do?" She sounded surprised.

"Yeah. I do. But sometimes, it's not easy to come to the same conclusions about things at the same time as another person," he said carefully. "Sometimes, when two people are at opposite ends of an issue, it's because one was able to move more quickly to the resolution than the other person. And that's what happened with us having a new baby. And the house. And sending Field away to school."

"Then you really meant what you said."

There was so much in her expression—gratitude tinged with hopelessness, and sadness laced with impregnable doubts that Stone didn't understand.

What did she want from him? What would it take to get her back?

He turned toward her, searching her eyes to measure the extent of her doubts. The chains of desire imprisoned him, held him fast, but his relationship with Dahlia was one of quicksand, forever shifting, changing beneath his feet.

Everything he'd ever loved and trusted—everything he'd ever counted on—was being torn away from him, and he was powerless to stop it. Dahlia had completely withdrawn from him, preferring to exist in a dream state, instead of in a world with him.

He knew—had known since her accident—that it was just Dahlia's way of coping with his emotional rejection on top of Brooke's death, that she was relying on her fantasy world for comfort instead of on him. And that hurt.

No doubt about it. It hurt like hell.

But Stone accepted the blame. He'd virtually abandoned their marriage after Brooke had died, forcing Dahlia to seek comfort elsewhere. Unfortunately that comfort came from believing she was an angel.

And now he honestly didn't know what to do. He'd offered her everything he had—but it wasn't working.

Why wasn't it working?

He grasped at the proverbial last straw with both hands. Leaning forward, he shoved his fingers through her hair and cupped her head. He had to try and prove to himself—and to her—that she still cared about him.

He needed her to still care about him. To care about them, their marriage, and their family.

He captured her mouth in a tender, deeply intimate kiss, demanding her silent acknowledgment that they were both alive and still wanted each other. And he got it.

But he was surprised when he pulled back and saw the shine of tears in her huge blue eyes.

"Dahlia...stay with me tonight." He took her cold hands in both of his and rubbed gently to warm them. "We don't have to do anything except talk, but—"

"I can't," she said softly. She looked down at her hands.

"Why?" When she didn't answer, Stone said quickly, "We have to talk about what's happened between us this year, why we turned away from each other at a time when we should have been close. Needed to be close."

The air fell deadly quiet, and it seemed like an eternity until her eyes lifted to meet his. The blue gaze was fearful.

"Look, this is the new-and-improved me," Stone said lightly. "No pressure, I swear. But until last spring, we had never slept apart except for when Brooke was born—and I don't like this. I miss you. I miss talking to you."

She smiled fleetingly at him, but remained painfully silent.

"Even a few weeks ago, you pushed and prodded me to face the future with open arms, to get on with our lives." He spoke slowly, carefully. "I'm willing to do that now, but you're not. Why? Why aren't you giving me a second chance? What *changed?*"

Something flashed in her eyes—hurt? anger? sorrow?— and then it was gone.

"I got tired of trying to get through to you," she said with devastating simplicity.

Stone let out a ragged breath in relief. He finally had an answer, one that had nothing to do with angels or getting into heaven or being with Brooke again.

"I know, honey," he said quickly, kissing the top of her head and drawing her gently to him. "And I'm sorry. I…I guess I fell back into my old way of dealing with things I can't change. Growing up on this all-male ranch, it was just easier to stuff things inside instead of talking about them."

"But our daughter was killed," Dahlia said against his shoulder.

Stone hugged her closer. "It'll be different this time, I swear. But you've got to help me with this. You've got to be willing to give me another chance. I can't do this alone, any more than you could this past year. We need to help each other through this."

She grew still in his arms, her face buried in his shoulder. And Stone wondered if she was thinking of herself as an angel with a mission tonight.

Magical thinking, the doctors called it? Wishing something to make it so? Dahlia must have been terrified to have reached this point—and he'd caused it.

He should have taken better care of her. He should have given her the baby she wanted, the instant she'd mentioned it. He should have…trusted her enough. Trusted her judgment. Dahlia was seldom wrong about things. She was the fearless one who had held on to life with both hands—even after Brooke died.

He was the damned coward in this family.

His heart and soul—his courage—had been buried along with his daughter.

"Dahlia," he said quietly, "it's time to let go of Brooke. It's time for both of us to let go of her, don't you see that? It's time you stopped living in Brooke's room and clinging to the past."

Dahlia lifted her head from his shoulder and pulled back, staring at him with intense concentration.

"It's time for me to stop clinging, too," he added with flat certainty.

"It's so hard to do." Her voice was barely a whisper, laced with such profound weariness, Stone suddenly made a decision.

"Would you stay in our room, if I slept somewhere else?" He had to get her out of Brooke's room, no matter what it took. Dahlia hesitated, started to say something, but he quickly shook his head, smiling at her. "It's okay. Come on, get into bed and go to sleep."

She followed him meekly and allowed him to tuck her into bed. He turned out the light and then bent to kiss her good-night. As he turned away, she grabbed his hand.

''I'm sorry,'' she said, her eyes fluttering closed.

''No, honey, I'm the one who's sorry,'' he answered, but she didn't hear him.

She was already asleep.

Chapter Seven

Dahlia stirred two cups of chopped pecans into the pancake batter the next morning. It was a Tyler family tradition to have pecan and blueberry pancakes every Saturday for breakfast, a tradition that had started the first morning she lived here.

It was the one part of Dahlia's family life that had not been abandoned since her daughter's death.

"Is it ready yet?" Shannon asked.

"Yeah, Mom, I'm starving to death!"

Field and Shannon climbed up on two stools on the opposite side of the island counter, watching as Dahlia spooned the batter into the skillet.

"As soon as these cook, we'll eat," she said, smiling inside. This, too, was a tradition. Children watching her cook, with the four Tyler men at the table, drinking coffee and talking. Flint and Shannon had shown up just in time for breakfast.

"Don't forget to make mine with blueberries," Shannon said.

"Yeah, me, too," Rocky called out.

"As if I haven't been doing this for nine years," Dahlia said lightly, sending an anxious glance in Stone's direction. Last night flashed briefly through her mind, his passion and tenderness—not to mention his patience—making her exceedingly nervous this morning.

Dahlia paused to take a sip of her morning coffee, holding back a sigh. This was always the best part of her week, and she wanted to savor every second of it.

She expertly flipped pancakes, sipped coffee and listened to the men discuss preparations for the approaching hurricane, but soon her mind was crowded with memories.

And thoughts of Stone.

Dahlia had longed for a home all those years she'd been shuffled from one Air Force base to another, dreaming of a kitchen like this one, crowded with family, with a husband and children to care for. She'd been blessed by the Tylers, who had drawn her instantly into their hearts.

And doubly blessed to have had Stone for a husband these past nine years.

"Aunt Dahlia?"

"Yes, sweetie?" she said absently, transferring the pancakes to a warm platter.

"Is it true Field doesn't have to go to that bad old school?"

"That bad old school is only one of the top boarding schools in the area." Flint had come up behind his daughter, reaching around her for the platter. "But you're right—it is old." He smiled at Dahlia.

"I know, Daddy, but Field couldn't live at home. And you said that's what he needed most—to live at home with Uncle Stone and Aunt Dahlia."

"Someone grab the syrup on the stove, please," Dahlia called over to the table, getting the platter of blueberry pancakes out of the oven, where she'd been keeping them warm. "And to answer your question, Shannon—yes. Field's staying on the ranch and going to school in Lemon Falls."

She didn't dare look at Stone. Evidently his brothers had their own opinions about Field going away to school, but this was the first she'd heard about it. She stole a glance in Stone's direction as he got up to help, too. But he didn't look upset.

"See, I told ya!" Field jumped down off the stool, following Flint over to the table.

"Ouch!" Rocky yelped, sucking his finger after dipping it into the maple syrup warming on top of the stove.

"It's hot." Dahlia grinned.

"No kidding." Rocky came around Dahlia, the pot in one hand as he searched for something to pour it in.

"Sweetie, here." Dahlia handed her brother-in-law a yellow ceramic gravy boat.

"I don't know why you always talk to me like I'm Shannon's age," Rocky complained. "Ouch!" he yelped again, smoldering a curse.

"Uncle Rocky, you're supposed to use a pot holder!" the little girl chirped over the general laughter in the room.

"I know that, little darling. I was just pretending to be stupid." He nursed his more recently wounded finger, while pouring the syrup into the gravy boat with his other hand.

Shannon looked confused, and Dahlia, coming around the island with the second platter of pancakes, whispered as she passed, "Uncle Rocky made a joke, sweetie."

Shannon followed her to the table, took her seat and reached for her napkin. Then, with perfect innocence, she said, "I'm getting a puppy."

Blade set the platter of sausages that Dahlia had cooked

earlier on the table. "A puppy?" He looked interested in his niece's comment.

Dahlia sat down at the table, while Stone provided glasses of juice and then poured more coffee for the adults. She glanced at Flint, who looked startled.

"What puppy, Shannon?" Flint asked his daughter.

"My puppy."

"She's talking about mine," Field chimed in. "She gets confused."

"I do not!"

Blade took his seat at the head of the table. "What are they talking about?" he asked, taking several pancakes and passing the platter to Dahlia.

There was a moment of uncomfortable silence as Blade waited for his question to be answered. Stone took his seat at the table, and Dahlia spoke before Stone could. "I thought Field should have one of Ginger's puppies. If that's okay with everybody."

Blade darted a glance in her direction, another toward Stone. Then his gaze came slowly back to her. "Uh... sure." He shrugged and started to eat.

"You're such a softy," Dahlia teased.

"Yeah, well, don't let it get around," Blade answered gruffly.

"Her name is Fluffy," Shannon went on as though there had been no conversation since her last comment.

"I already told you ten times," Field said sternly, "the puppy's name is Tiger Rose—*not Fluffy!*"

"Field—" Stone warned.

"Don't talk to Shannon like that," Dahlia said at the same time.

"Yeah, but she's always getting things wrong—"

"Just 'cause you know how to read and write and I don't doesn't mean I'm dumb!" Shannon announced.

Stone and Flint were trying not to grin. Rocky laughed outright, then nearly choked when Shannon glared at him.

"Of course it doesn't, sweetie," Dahlia said soothingly, shaking her head reprovingly at her youngest brother-in-law.

"As soon as you start first grade, honey, they'll teach you how to read," Blade added quickly.

"Which is only in a week or so," her father added.

"Aunt Dahlia?"

"What, sweetie?"

"Please don't call me sweetie anymore," Shannon said seriously.

Dahlia was surprised. "Okay. But why?"

"Because I'm a big girl now."

A big girl. Those three little words hit Dahlia in the heart. Brooke had also rebelled at the strangest things when she was six. When the whole idea of entering the exciting, terrifying world of first grade was beginning to sink in.

"Hey, what's wrong with being called sweetie?" Rocky asked his little niece. "Dahlia calls me that lots of times."

Dahlia smiled across the table at Rocky, watching him give Shannon another blueberry pancake. But all she could see was the empty place where Brooke should have been.

"I know plenty of stuff," Shannon said importantly.

"Yeah, like what?" Field said with pure ten-year-old male superiority.

Dahlia felt Stone's worried gaze the instant it landed on her, and she quickly took a huge bite of her pancake, pretending she was very hungry. Even with the hurricane rapidly approaching, she felt safe sitting here at this big round kitchen table where she was surrounded by the people she loved.

Except…except one of those people was gone for good.

"I know about the cav—" Shannon started to say, only to be smoothly interrupted by Field.

"You can name the puppy Fluffy if you want to," Field told her hastily. "I don't care."

"I didn't name your puppy Fluffy. I named my puppy Fluffy!"

"What?" Three Tyler men asked the question at once.

Shannon sat up straight in her chair and looked around the table. "If Field gets a puppy, then so do I," she said with touching logic.

Dahlia watched the four men exchange rueful glances.

"What do you think?" Blade asked Flint.

Flint sighed and looked at his daughter. "Okay, but the puppy—"

"Fluffy," Shannon supplied.

"Fluffy will have to stay on the ranch—"

"No!" Shannon wailed.

"Just fence in your backyard. I'll help you one weekend," Rocky offered.

"I'll help, too," Field chimed in.

"The four of us can fence in your yard in a day," Blade added. He looked at Field and smiled. "The five of us."

Dahlia smiled to herself at the way they all jumped in to help each other. Field was going to be all right. And so was Stone. They had the rest of the family. They didn't need her.

She sighed heavily. Maybe if she kept telling herself that, in time she'd believe it. Because needing someone had very little to do with loving another person and then losing them.

That is, if Stone still loved her.

Sometimes she just wasn't sure.

Sometimes she thought all his love for her had been buried along with Brooke. And what hadn't been buried had been eaten up by grief and silent rage.

The men had finished eating, and Dahlia brushed off their attempts to help her clean up the kitchen. They had a lot of work to get done today. The latest bulletin from the weather channel indicated the hurricane was headed straight toward Lemon Falls.

She looked outside. It had stopped raining. As the men left by the back door, a blast of hot, humid air entered the kitchen. The calm before the storm, Dahlia thought with a sigh, feeling restless and uneasy.

She poured herself another cup of coffee and listened to the children's excited chatter about their new puppies. But Dahlia couldn't keep her mind on what they were saying.

She was thinking too much, remembering too much about what it had been like being married to Stone, making love with him. And total desolation, like an icy wind off the ocean, permeated her bones. All morning she'd felt Stone's eyes straying toward her, a gaze filled with yearning and need.

And she told herself sharply it was just sexual yearning. Nothing more. Nothing less.

Because that part of him hadn't died. The part that had died had to do with little things like love and trust and faith. It had to do with shutting down inside and completely shutting her out of his life.

Dahlia sipped her coffee, unwilling to get up and clear the table just yet. Why had it taken him this long to come to his senses? *Why* had he waited until yesterday before seeing what she'd known all along? Why on earth was Stone doing this to her now?

When she no longer had a choice in the matter.

But you do have a choice, a tiny voice in her head said clearly. *Basil merely warned you that if you didn't complete your mission and return within the scheduled time, then you couldn't go through the gate. He didn't say you had to return, now did he?*

No, but that was what he'd meant!

He only meant that if you wanted to go through the gate and be with Brooke, then you had to restore Stone's faith before next Friday, the tiny voice persisted. *He never said what would happen if you failed.*

What *would* happen if she failed? Dahlia wondered uncertainly. What if she decided to stay?

Could she stay?

Her head began to hurt again. Before, she'd accepted Basil's mission on blind faith. But now she had more questions than answers.

Doubt wormed its way past her defenses. Was she truly an angel, or was Stone right? Was she hiding behind being an angel so she wouldn't have to accept Brooke's death?

No. She was an angel!

If that's true, then why haven't you gone through the gate?

Damn—uh, darn! she thought unhappily, thinking the little voice in her head sounded too much like Stone's. Darn his logic, anyway!

She hadn't gone through the gate because it wasn't time yet. The hurricane would provide the answers. It had to be a sign from Basil, so all she had to do was wait.

Dahlia got up and hurriedly cleared the table, loaded the dishwasher and wiped off the counters. Didn't anyone realize how hard this was for her? How hard this whole year had been? Trying desperately to hold her marriage together all by herself? With little help from Stone.

And now, just because he had decided it was time to resume their lives together, she was supposed to fall in with his plans?

When pigs fly!

"Aunt Dahlia?" a timid little voice said.

"What is it, Shannon?"

"Mom, are you mad or something?" Field was staring at her from the kitchen table, his gray eyes wide and concerned.

"No, of course not," she said impatiently.

"Then why are you slamming things around?"

Dahlia was startled. And ashamed. Shannon looked on the verge of tears, making her feel even worse. What in heaven's name was wrong with her this morning? she wondered, tossing aside her dish towel and approaching the two children.

Hugging them, she said, "I guess the hurricane's making me nervous. I'm sorry." And then she added quickly, "What do you say we go and look at your new puppies?"

That suggestion was greeted by a cheer, and Dahlia followed them to the door, her thoughts still spinning. Being with the children was a wonderful distraction, and she planned to make the most of the time she had left.

But somewhere deep inside she wondered if she had to leave them, if she actually had a choice to go or to stay. And a little voice whispered, *They all need you just as much as they ever did. You're letting fear drive you away. Stone's giving you another chance to make things right for your family. Why don't you take it?*

Ignoring the irritating little voice, Dahlia crossed the yard toward the barn, and Shannon slipped her little hand into hers. Trusting her to always be there for her, as an aunt and a friend. Field ran ahead, but Dahlia noticed he'd paused by the barn door and turned around, making sure she was coming with him.

Field expected her to come with him, to see the puppies, to always be there for him, too. She was the only mother he had ever known, and he would need her so much the next few years, even though he'd never admit it.

When Dahlia reached the door, Field captured her free hand in his and playfully pulled her inside the barn. The three of them silently observed the sleeping puppies in the corner, but soon Shannon grew bored by the inactivity of Fluffy and Tiger Rose, and drifted off to find a picture book she'd left in the barn weeks ago. Dahlia and Field sat quietly together for several minutes before he spoke.

"Thanks, Mom." His voice was soft and low and he kept his gaze on the puppies.

"For Tiger Rose?"

"For...everything." He looked up at her quickly, but then his gaze darted away again. "For making Dad let me stay here."

Dahlia sighed inwardly. "It was his decision, sweetie. I can't take credit for it." She still wasn't certain what had caused the swift change in Stone.

"You changed his mind," Field insisted. "I know you did. You can do anything."

That statement hurt her more than anything he could have said.

Because, in truth, she couldn't do enough. Hadn't she proven it to herself over and over again this past year? All her efforts to fix her marriage, to fix her life, had fallen on deaf ears.

"I'm glad you think so, sweetie. But adults can't fix everything."

Field looked at her and then slid his hand into hers. He hesitated before saying, "It wasn't your fault Brooke died."

Dahlia jerked her head around, and their gazes locked hard. And just for an instant, the clear, honest gray eyes looking into hers were the eyes of a man. The eyes of his father.

"Brooke disobeyed you. And she knew better, too." He was studying his tennis shoes now. "I told her and told her not to go near Firelight by herself, that she was too little, but she wasn't thinking that morning, Mom. She just did it."

Dahlia dragged in a breath and released it quickly, not knowing what to say.

But Field didn't give her a chance to say anything, for he stated flatly, "Dad thinks it was all his fault, doesn't he?"

"Yes." Dahlia's reply was honest. "I'm afraid he does." She expected more questions, but Field remained silent.

A few moments later Shannon came back from her search and skipped happily over to them. "I found it!" she announced. "Look at it with me, please, Aunt Dahlia?"

"I'll look at it with you," Field offered.

Shannon scrambled between them and sat down. Dahlia's heart was full of love for both children as she watched them, their heads almost touching, as they looked through the picture book.

Stone walked over to the corral, hoisted himself onto the split-rail fence and took off his light gray Stetson, battered by years of use. The heat and humidity was getting to him, and he took several deep, slow breaths. He untied the red bandanna he'd been using as a sweatband, wrung it out and spread it across the fence to dry.

He looked up at the sky and blew out a breath. They were now under a "hurricane watch," which meant they were in probable danger of being hit within twenty-four hours. He looked at his watch. It was early afternoon. That meant all hell could break loose before this time tomorrow.

If they were at all lucky, it wouldn't hit until morning. If it hit at all.

Blade came up to him and handed Stone a cold glass of lemonade.

"Where did you get this?" Stone asked.

"On the front porch. Dahlia has sandwiches, too." Without further explanation, Blade handed him a chicken sandwich, wrapped in a napkin.

"Thanks." Stone took a thirsty swallow of the lemonade, uneasy about how hard Dahlia was working today. But their cook had gone into town with Rocky for extra supplies and wasn't back yet.

"Flint found that case of batteries you were looking for," Blade said, the casual comment a direct contrast to the searching way his brother was studying him. "And the extra flashlights."

Stone was too hot and tired to eat, so he merely contented himself with the lemonade. He could hear the talk and laughter coming from the front porch, knowing the men were taking a much-needed lunch break, and Stone listened to them happily chatting with Dahlia.

The men adored his wife. Dahlia was the undisputed mistress of Tyler Ranch and had been from the beginning. Her warmth and friendliness spilled over onto everyone who met her, young and old alike.

If there were such things as angels on earth, Stone thought softly, he knew Dahlia had the right stuff to be one. She was unfailingly good and kind, always positive and happy, filled with energy and good will.

Until he'd single-handedly destroyed all that by burying himself in grief this past year.

"You did the right thing by letting Field stay on the ranch," Blade was saying. "The right thing for all three of you."

Stone shrugged. "He's a little boy. He needs his family now."

Blade started to say something else, then stopped and looked away. Silence fell between them, and Stone wondered if his brother sensed things hadn't been resolved between him and Dahlia.

To cover up what he was feeling, Stone said, "It'll take some time, but things will be back to normal pretty soon."

"Good," was all Blade had to say about it.

They talked briefly about the afternoon's hurricane preparations that they'd already discussed. Stone had the curious feeling that Blade was hanging around, making himself available if Stone needed to talk. And Stone started to, only something held him back.

Loyalty to Dahlia, perhaps?

Or maybe he just wasn't ready to admit to any of his brothers what a total mess he'd made out of marriage—once again.

The first time, he'd been too young to recognize a gold digger when he'd married one. Dahlia was the complete opposite of his first wife.

But he'd still failed in every major way with her, too.

After Blade gave up and left him alone, Stone ate the sandwich and drained his glass of lemonade. He sat uneasily on the top rail of the fence and wondered what to do next.

One of the doctors at the hospital had suggested that Dahlia's grim determination to move forward with building the new house and having another baby could have been a form of denial. By insisting they go on with their plans as though Brooke hadn't been killed, Dahlia hadn't embraced the future as much as tried to erase the past.

The doctor also believed Dahlia had never truly grieved for Brooke—and neither had Stone.

Stone looked up when he heard someone approaching, and smiled at his young son. Field was walking toward him, carrying a second glass of lemonade. Stone slid off the fence just as Field thrust the glass out for him to take.

"I thought you'd like some more," his son said shyly.

"I would. Thanks." Stone took a sip of the lemonade and silently regarded his son. It wasn't right that his own flesh and blood was this tentative around him. He didn't use to be, but Stone wasn't sure if this change in him was because Field was growing up, or because of this past year.

"You think the puppies will be safe in the barn?" Field asked him.

"I expect so." Field was looking up at him expectantly, so Stone elaborated, "We've been through hurricanes before."

"But they haven't."

"Ginger will take care of her puppies."

"Who's going to take care of Ginger?"

Stone put his hand on his son's shoulder. "We're doing all we can to secure the ranch from possible damage, and to protect everyone who lives here from harm—and that includes all the animals. But you already know that, so what's really bothering you?"

"Tiger Rose and Fluffy are real little." The gray eyes, so like his own, stared up at Stone. "They're going to be so scared. And I was thinking…you said Tiger Rose could move into my room—"

"We can't take Tiger Rose away from her mother until she's weaned," Stone patiently explained. "Or Fluffy, either. Those puppies are less than two days old. They'll be safe in the barn," he added gently.

Field lowered his eyes to the ground and kicked at the dirt with the tip of his black high-top jogging shoe. "I know. I'm only asking 'cause Shannon's worried about Fluffy. I told her I'd ask you about it.''

Stone hid a smile. ''That was very considerate of you. It's good that you're taking care of her.''

''Yeah, well...'' He squirmed uncomfortably. ''I'm the only brother she's got, even though she's my cousin.''

Stone grew still. ''And big brothers take care of their little sisters,'' he stated softly, thinking of the way Field had always looked after Brooke and Shannon.

Field stared at the ground for a long time without saying anything. And then he said hesitantly, ''I was wondering if...you thought Brooke was...was...''

''If Brooke was what?'' Stone held his breath, waiting, not knowing what to expect.

''If Brooke was okay.'' After a second or two had passed, Field looked up quickly, as though to see if Stone was going to get angry. ''In...heaven.''

''There is nothing you can't say to me, Field,'' Stone gently prompted, sensing there was much more coming.

Field took a deep breath and let it out in a terrible rush. ''This guy in my class last year said there was nothing but darkness when you die, that there isn't any heaven. Brooke was scared of the dark.''

Stone felt as if all the air had suddenly been knocked out of his lungs. ''People believe different things about death,'' he slowly answered. ''Some believe that when you die, that's it. You don't feel anything, so there is no pain or fear. Sort of like being born. You can't remember being born, can you?''

Field shook his head, his expression intent.

''That's passing from one life into the next one, without being aware of it.''

''But you're somewhere after you're born,'' Field protested.

Stone smiled at him. "Other people believe that when you die you go to heaven. And you can sit back and eat all the hot fudge sundaes you want without having to worry about fat content or high cholesterol or anything else. Brooke is okay, no matter where she is," he added swiftly.

"But if there's no heaven—"

"If there is no heaven, she isn't aware of anything, so she can't possibly be afraid. But," Stone added quickly, "if there is a heaven, then she's having a great time putting tons of icing on her chocolate cake and eating as many goodies as she wants."

There was a moment's silence.

"Which do you believe, Dad?" He was practically holding his breath, anxiously waiting for Stone's answer.

Stone looked directly at his son and spoke the truth. "I believe she's in heaven, sitting on the front porch with your grandparents—my parents, the ones you and Brooke never had the chance to meet—and they're spoiling her in a major way."

Relief flashed through Field's eyes. "That's what I believe, too."

Stone ruffled his son's dark hair affectionately, thinking how small Field was for his age. But he'd grow up all too soon. And Stone suddenly realized how much time he'd wasted this past year, time he should have spent with the child he had left.

The child who'd needed him the most.

The child who'd had to live with the fact of his sister's death—without his father's help.

"I miss her, Dad." Field's voice was low, as though he was ashamed to admit to that kind of weakness.

"I know," Stone said, drawing his son toward him. "I miss her, too." He swallowed hard. "But everything will be okay now. I'll see to it that your life is as good as it was before we lost Brooke.''

The vow he made to Field was also one he was making to himself.

''Stone!'' Flint was waving at him from the corner of the house. ''It's official. A hurricane warning went into effect a moment ago!''

That meant the storm was definitely coming through here in less than twenty-four hours. Stone waved to his brother to let him know he'd heard and noticed Dahlia was behind him. For an instant their gazes locked uncertainly, and then she turned away.

Chapter Eight

Dahlia stared at the ceiling in the room she'd once shared with Stone. She glanced at the clock on the night table and sighed. It was just before dawn. She might as well get up. Dahlia knew her inability to sleep tonight had little to do with the hurricane that would be here in a few hours.

It had everything to do with being back in this room the past two nights, in this bed, without Stone.

Dahlia sat up, hugging herself as she glanced toward the bay window. The wind was slamming into the house, and, according to the most recent news report, the hurricane hadn't reached inland yet. But everyone was settled down for the night. She wondered how the rest of the family could sleep through this.

Of course, the Tyler family was used to hurricanes. But Dahlia had never gotten used to them. Not really.

The ranch was as secure as they could make it. They were far enough inland so the hurricane wouldn't have the same force when it hit as it would on the Gulf. On the other hand, they were less than two hundred miles from the coast.

And the hurricane promised to be a monster.

She quickly pulled on a pair of jeans and a shirt and slipped her bare feet into canvas, rubber-soled shoes. She was going to make a pot of coffee and just stay up. Maybe downstairs she wouldn't feel quite so empty and alone.

Dahlia took the back steps down to the kitchen and made herself a pot of her favorite chocolate-macadamia-nut coffee that the others intensely disliked. Sipping the hot, soothing liquid, she tried to relax. She'd survived a lot of bad storms and hurricanes since she'd arrived in Texas. She'd get through this one, too.

But would she get through the loss of Stone and Field and any future children she might have had?

At some point during the hurricane, would Basil send for her? She had done all she could to restore Stone's faith in himself.

Now the only thing she could do was wait.

Dahlia cradled the oversize coffee cup with both hands, forcibly removing all thought from her mind. She was so tired of thinking and feeling, and more than tired of talking. All she wanted was some peace and quiet.

But she soon discovered her thoughts kept following a path into the faraway past, to the beginning of her relationship with Stone. At a time when he'd wanted to marry her, but had been scared of that kind of commitment. It had taken a great deal of faith on his part to trust his heart to her after his first wife had left him.

Dahlia propped her elbows on the table and buried her face in her hands. Her head was beginning to hurt again, and she gently massaged both temples, looking for release from the pain. She didn't want to abandon Stone or Field. She loved them. She'd always loved them.

She just wanted to be with her daughter.

Her thoughts skidded back farther into the past, to all

those years of moving around when she was growing up, of never having a real home. She'd vowed that one day she'd have a daughter and nothing would ever hurt her little girl. Not loneliness or despair. And not a moment's pain or discomfort. She'd vowed to see to it personally.

But she hadn't.

She'd allowed her daughter to be killed.

The pain in her head was getting worse. Dahlia got up to take half a pain pill the doctor had prescribed, enough to take the edge off. Then she poured herself a second cup of caffeine-laced coffee and sat alone, sipping it slowly.

She jumped once when the wind slammed into the kitchen windows, making the windowpanes rattle. She decided then to get her book out of the living room and sit at the breakfast nook until dawn. Reading was always a good way to get her mind off things she'd rather not be thinking about.

Like the frightening thought of the hurricane.

Or—more to the point—the terrifying thought of Stone and how it had felt last night when he'd kissed her. The memory of the way he'd felt and smelled and tasted filled Dahlia with a sudden wave of sheer, healthy lust. She remembered the way his rough, callused hands had warmed hers, so strong and gentle and soothing.

The same magical hands that had the exquisite ability to—

Dahlia blocked the tantalizing memory half forming in her mind and stood up. Maybe it was the threatening approach of the hurricane getting to her, making her remember things she was trying so hard to forget.

But as she headed toward the front of the house, all she could feel was the awesome responsibility of love.

She turned the light on in the front hall and pushed open

one of the double doors leading to the living room—and
stopped in her tracks.

Stone was sitting on one of the love seats situated at right
angles to the fireplace, with only the lamplight near him to
chase away the darkness in the room. He looked up, startled, when the light poured in from the hall, and Dahlia
hesitated.

She should have remembered, but she hadn't. Stone was
usually up early when there was a hurricane warning. The
radio was on the coffee table, turned down low. Stone was
fully dressed except for his boots. But they were sitting
side by side next to the table.

Everything felt so familiar—and right.

The two of them alone downstairs while the rest of the
family slept. The wind and rain hammering the house with
increasing force, yet, inside, they were all safe and warm
and…together.

Like a family.

Her family.

Dahlia switched off the hall light and closed the door
behind her, thinking she should just leave him alone. But
somehow she couldn't. Something drew her into the room.
A memory of cherished times in the past. A feeling of
safety. Of feeling whole and complete.

It was fleeting, but it was there.

She felt his surprised gaze following her as she came
into the room and sat down on the love seat facing him.
Three blue-and-yellow-flowered love seats formed a square
with the fireplace, with a large blue rug in the middle. A
rug that was incredibly soft.

And she should know. She'd made love with Stone on
this blue rug more than once when the family was away.
And sometimes in the middle of the night, while the family

was tucked away upstairs, they'd lock those double doors and shut out the world.

The wind slammed into a window and she jumped, startled. Okay, not on nights like this one, she remembered somewhat giddily. They'd never made love with a bad storm approaching, much less a rip-roaring hurricane.

A faint grin appeared on Stone's face, but his gaze was gentle as it rested on her. "You okay?"

"Sure. Why wouldn't I be?" she said a little *too* quickly.

Stone's grin broadened. "No reason. Just wondering."

Dahlia noticed a flashlight beside the radio, with extra batteries. She'd left her flashlight upstairs, which was foolish to do during a hurricane warning. The power could go out at any second.

"I made some coffee. It's mine, but I could make you a pot of straight coffee," she offered. "Would you like a cup?"

Stone shook his head. "No, thanks. I had some earlier." His eyes never left her face. "I'm wired enough as it is."

"What's the latest news?" she asked nervously.

"It should hit us mid-morning," he answered.

"I came down for my book." She looked around until she spotted it on the long, narrow table behind the love seat. "I didn't think anybody else was up."

"I'm always up tracking a hurricane. You know that." There was that same even tone of voice he'd been using a lot with her lately. And that same cool, remote expression suddenly in his gaze.

A gaze that solidly refused to budge from watching her face.

"I forgot," she replied.

Dahlia floundered for something else to say to him. The silence bothered her, although she thought she heard something in another part of the house. She listened intently for a moment, but all she heard was a fresh gust of wind ramming into the front of the house. She hugged herself.

Boy, her nerves were shot!

She was uncomfortable being alone downstairs with Stone, especially when he appeared to have slipped back into being silent and distant toward her. Oh, dear, was he slipping back into his old ways? Was he shutting her out again? Or was he simply preoccupied with the approaching hurricane?

Her gaze landed on the television in the corner of the room. "Have you been watching the weather channel?"

Stone shrugged. "I turn it on every half hour or so."

Dahlia sighed and then demanded, "Are you shutting me out again?"

"Shutting you out?" Stone looked confused.

"The way you've been doing this past year. Becoming silent and distant and—"

"Dahlia, look, everything is okay. Nothing has changed." He said it slowly and carefully, as though talking to a complete and total half-wit.

"You needn't take that tone with me," Dahlia said irritably.

He almost smiled. "What tone?"

"That patient tone that men use with women they think are silly and beyond belief. Field used it with Shannon this morning."

"Ah, the puppy dilemma." Stone cracked a quick smile then, one that rapidly turned into a grin.

"I guess we put Blade on the spot in more ways than one," Dahlia said sheepishly. "Is he very angry?"

He shrugged. "No more so than Flint." Then Stone laughed. "He was grumbling all day about having no time to take proper care of a new puppy."

Dahlia sighed. "Then I guess I have two apologies to make."

"This ranch belongs to you as much as it does to them," he told her slowly. "And that includes everything on it. If you decide to give our son one of Ginger's puppies, then it's fine with me. And my brothers. You know that."

Dahlia still felt guilty about the puppies. "But they're terribly expensive purebreds. Good herding dogs—not pets," she protested.

"Ginger had nine babies. Blade can spare two of them for the kids."

"But Flint does have a hectic schedule and—"

Stone waved aside her concern. "Give him a day or two and he'll love the idea. Besides, little girls need puppies to love as much as little boys."

"And their own horses, too," she murmured, and then looked quickly at him, horrified by what she had said. Why on earth had she said that?

But Stone was nodding in agreement. "Horses, too."

A tight silence stretched between them, like a bridge each one was unwilling to cross just yet. They both feared it wouldn't hold the weight of their combined grief.

Dahlia quickly skidded toward a safer topic. "I think I'll take Field into San Antonio next Saturday and buy him his new schoolclothes, and the other things he'll need."

Stone looked surprised, then nodded. "I'm sure he'll like that."

"We'll make a day of it," she added eagerly. "We'll go shopping and have lunch at River Walk." The city's famous River Walk, winding along the San Antonio River past restaurants, stores, flower gardens and stately pecan trees, was a favorite treat for Field. "After lunch we'll check out that dinosaur exhibit at Witt Museum he's been wanting to see—"

Dahlia broke off uncertainly, not knowing what to do or which way to look. What was she doing? She couldn't do any of those things with Field because she wouldn't be here! She wouldn't be here to watch her son grow up!

How could she have possibly forgotten?

Dahlia felt her hands beginning to tremble and quickly clasped them together. She'd forgotten, for a brief, sweet moment, that things weren't the same.

How could she have forgotten?

What kind of a mother was she to have completely forgotten about Brooke, even for an instant?

The wind once again battered the front of the house and Dahlia jumped, cried out and buried her face in her hands.

"Dahlia, what is it?" Stone was already off the love seat and circling the square coffee table. "What's wrong?"

"N-nothing."

"Don't give me that." He sounded slightly impatient and more than a little concerned. He sat down next to her and put his arm around her. "Talk to me. Tell me what you're thinking," he prompted.

Dahlia gave a quick shake of her head. She was loath to bring up any topic concerning her mission or anything else tonight. It just felt too...too comfortable and peaceful in here to risk another fight with him.

Besides, how could she explain when she didn't understand it herself? How could she explain how wonderfully normal it felt being in this room with Stone tonight? As though the entire last year had never happened.

How could she explain that it had felt so normal that she'd completely forgotten her mission—and getting back to Brooke! What kind of person was she to have forgotten? What kind of mother? Guilt raged through her, frantic and menacing.

"You're shaking." Stone's arm tightened around her.

Another huge gust of wind hit the front door and Dahlia spun toward him, burying her face against his throat, her fingers grabbing at his shirt. Why was she still frightened of storms? she wondered. She was an angel, wasn't she? How could she still be so frightened?

Stone held her as she shivered, and suddenly she was five years old again, in a strange new place, in the middle of a terrible tropical storm, with only the new housekeeper for company. A young woman who didn't speak English very well and who couldn't understand why Dahlia had been frightened.

Dahlia shuddered once and pulled back. "I'm sorry."

Stone brushed her hair back from her face with gentle fingers. "For what? Being afraid of storms? I've never held that against you, have I? So why do you think I'd start now?"

She gazed uncertainly up at him. The tender concern in his gray eyes made her lose all track of her thoughts. All she could see was Stone.

And all she could remember was how it felt for him to touch her, kiss her—and make love with her.

Stone's eyes searched her face, his gaze softening, deepening, almost as though he'd read her mind. He bent his head and kissed her, and when his mouth took hers, Dahlia felt something give way deep in her chest. Like soft earth crumbling after a heavy rain.

The kiss lengthened and deepened and blended hungrily into another and another— But she couldn't do this!

She couldn't make love with him!

If she did, then she'd never have the strength to leave him, and she'd never see Brooke again!

She couldn't have Stone and Field, and Brooke, too. It went against the rules. Dahlia gently disengaged herself from Stone's embrace and glanced around uneasily.

"What's wrong?" Stone asked.

"The creaking noises in this old house are giving me the creeps!"

"It's probably the wind," he said soothingly.

Dahlia shrugged. Everything seemed to be closing in on her, and she couldn't breathe. And her head was hurting again. It had eased somewhat, but now it was beginning to pound.

Stone looked worried. "Do you want me to light the fire? You look cold."

Dahlia shook her head, even though she was hugging herself. "It's August. Too hot for a fire," she said, feeling cranky and edgy again.

"Talk to me. Tell me how you feel."

"I don't want to talk. Or think. Or feel. I just want to be left alone," she said resignedly.

"Yeah, right, whenever we start getting close, you start backing off," Stone drawled out.

Something in Dahlia snapped.

"If I remember correctly, you're the one who was always backing off!" she blurted out. "Backing away from us, our marriage and our son. We needed you, damn it!"

"Did you just use a swear word?"

Dahlia was horrified. Did she? She couldn't remember. But the grin on Stone's face made her want to use a few more—a few choice ones, too!

His grin had broadened. "Feels good to hear you swear. Haven't seen much of the real you lately. Haven't heard the real you, either."

Dahlia wanted to wipe that grin off his face. Instead she stood up and paced around the room.

Stone watched her stalk the room for several seconds. "Dahlia, I'm sorry I teased you," he said finally. He sounded as though he meant it.

"No, I'm sorry," she said quickly. "I shouldn't have said any of that."

She needed to move. She needed to run, but where could she go?

"Why can't you just say what you feel without apologizing for it?" His low voice was filled with barely restrained frustration. He stood up and walked toward her. "We used to talk about everything. Our first date we stayed up all night talking, or have you forgotten?" he asked, stepping in front of her as she tried to brush past him.

She stopped and looked at him. "No, I haven't forgotten." There was an unspoken accusation tacked on to the end of her sentence that Stone couldn't possibly have missed.

And he didn't. "I haven't forgotten, either," he told her softly. "I know I should have talked to you about what I was feeling after Brooke died, but—"

"It doesn't matter now."

There was a sudden, deafening silence between them. "How can you stand there and say that to me?" Stone's voice suddenly shook with pent-up emotion. "How can it not matter when our lives are falling to pieces all around us?"

"But if you'd only let me fix it, everything would be okay!" she burst out. "If you'd only believe I'm an angel—"

He groaned and closed his eyes, shaking his head slightly.

"I'm telling you the truth, but if you can't see it, then hey, it's not real."

"Dahlia, I know it's real to you," he said slowly. "I know something happened when you were in that coma...."

"But?" Dahlia waited.

His expression was grave. "But there are no such things as angels."

"How do you know that?"

"Because believing in angels is taking the easy way out," he answered gently. "It takes the responsibility for our actions off our own shoulders and puts it where it doesn't belong."

Dahlia stared up at him for a long, painful moment. She felt so hurt that he didn't believe her, that she hadn't restored his faith. "Don't you believe in anything, Stone?" she asked.

"I believe what I was taught—that you have to help yourself. I believe I didn't do such a great job this whole last year in that department," he added quickly. "And I believe I hurt you in ways that I'm only just now beginning to realize."

"But you don't believe what's happened to me," she stated sadly.

"No. I don't." He said it regretfully. Dahlia gave him that. But it wasn't going to help her get back to Brooke.

She started to turn away. "Then I have nothing left to say to you." She had failed. She knew that now—and she was out of time.

Stone grabbed her hand. "Sweetheart, listen to me. We have to talk this out. We need to talk about what you're feeling, what you're doing to our lives—"

Dahlia yanked her hand out of his. "You're the one who gave Brooke—" She managed to break off the hurtful comment in time, but she also knew Stone realized what she had been about to say.

She watched shock hit him like a bullet, and she knew she'd fired the shot.

"Stone, I'm sorry." Dahlia appeared to Stone as though she wished the floor would open up and swallow her whole.

"I didn't mean it. I don't believe it. I'm not even supposed to say things like that. Or even think them."

Stone became angry then. No, more than angry. He was absolutely furious. Not because of the accusation, but because Dahlia refused to talk to him about the way she felt. She kept hiding behind the subject of angels whenever they got anywhere near the truth.

Or whenever they started to get close to each other again. What in the hell was she afraid of?

Stone had tried to be patient with this angel business, but his patience was wearing thin. Dahlia wasn't cooperating at all—and everything was at stake. Their present. Their future. And even their past. Because how could they hope to remember the good times with Brooke and with each other, if all they remembered was the pain and grief and guilt?

"It's okay," Stone told her evenly, his anger fading as quickly as it had hit. "I know you thought Brooke was too young for a horse of her own."

"I didn't mean—"

Stone brushed off her protest. "That's exactly what you meant," he said stiffly. "And you were right. She was too young. And Firelight was too high-spirited. I should have listened to you. But I didn't and now she's gone, and I'm sorry. But there's nothing I can do about it now," he added roughly. "I can't fix it. I can't bring her back. But one thing I sure as hell do know—believing you're an angel is not helping this situation one damn bit. Hiding behind—"

"I'm not hiding!"

"We need to talk about it, Dahlia. We need to help each other get over Brooke's death."

"You expect me to get over Brooke's death?" Dahlia looked at him incredulously.

Stone gripped her hands. "Not her death, but the guilt," he said, taking a deep, ragged breath. "We need to help each other get over the guilt and the pain and the grief."

Dahlia was shaking her head while he was speaking, making him more and more nervous.

"It's not a weakness to reach out for help when you need it. You used to tell me that all the time."

She sighed softly. "It's not that simple."

"Yes, it is."

"If you would just believe me about Basil—"

"And if you would only trust me!"

She gripped his hands tightly. "What about faith? Isn't that what faith is—believing in something you can't explain? Trusting in something that you can't see or hear, something beyond belief, yet knowing it's there?"

Her blue eyes were wide and clear, free of doubt, and he gazed at each fine curve and line of the beloved features that had been indelibly sketched upon the inside of his eyelids, night after sleepless night, the past twelve months.

And he struggled to put it together in his mind, but it was too much all at once.

He believed Dahlia needed to stop hiding behind her fantasy of being an angel, and properly deal with Brooke's death.

And Dahlia thought she needed him to believe in angels, or she'd never see Brooke again.

"Answer me!" Dahlia cried. "What does faith mean to you?"

He searched her face. He had no answers he could give her. None that made sense, anyway. Dahlia had always seen things in black or white, with no gray areas. She did nothing halfway. If she believed she was an angel, then she was—end of discussion.

Stone's sigh was heavy. "I have faith in us—in you and me. In our marriage."

"And yet you lost your faith after Brooke died," she pointed out with a shrug.

"I didn't think you'd understand." His voice was low, uncertain.

"You didn't think I'd understand how you felt?" Dahlia was astounded. "Your daughter was killed. *Our* daughter was killed. What did you think I wouldn't understand?"

Stone hesitated. "Do you know what my father did the night my mom died?" When Dahlia shook her head, he said, "He went into the library and did the payroll. When I asked him why he couldn't wait, he said the men had earned their pay and were expecting the checks to be handed out the next morning. And that's exactly what he did. The same thing he'd always done on the last day of each and every month."

Dahlia watched him carefully.

"He loved my mother more than…anything. But he had a ranch to run and bills to pay, not to mention four kids to raise. Rocky and Flint hadn't started school yet, and Blade and I were in the fifth and sixth grades." Stone looked at her. "Do you want to know what I did when my father died? I helped Flint with his geometry and fixed Rocky's bicycle."

Dahlia met his gaze unflinchingly and understood now why he hadn't talked to her after Brooke died. Stone hadn't had the slightest idea how.

"I'm sorry."

"For what?"

"Oh…" She glanced out the window. "For assuming too much, I suppose."

Stone's grin was fleeting. "Why did you think I didn't talk to you?"

She looked at him. "I thought you didn't need me."

"Dahlia—"

But she was shaking her head. "It doesn't matter now."

"It does matter," he stated flatly. "Why do you keep saying it doesn't?"

Dahlia started to move past him, but he grabbed her by the hand. As soon as he touched her, she jerked back, as though burned.

"Damn it, why do you do that?" Stone's voice was low and flat and hollow.

"Do what?"

"Pull back when we start connecting."

Dahlia pushed her way past him and started to pace. "Because it's...it's..." If she said it was too late, Stone would explode. She knew he would. She whirled on him. "Stone, why don't you believe I was at the gates of heaven? Why don't you believe I saw Brooke? Why don't you believe Basil sent me here to help us?"

"Help us?" Stone jumped on the word like a cat on a mouse. "I thought you said Basil sent you back here to help me?"

"He...he did." Dahlia was flustered, unsure of what she'd meant by the remark. But she rallied in the face of his disbelief. "Helping you will help me. That's what I meant."

Stone spit out a low, rough expletive. Something like Yeah, when pigs fly.

Only...not as polite.

Dahlia decided to try another approach. "When have I ever lied to you?"

"I know you're not lying to me." Stone glanced up, and their gazes tangled for a moment. "You're just... confused."

"Stone…" What could she say to him that would make sense? "I need you to believe me."

"And if I can't?" Brutal pain entered his gray eyes. "What then? What if I can't believe what you're telling me?" His voice was soft and low. "What will you do then?"

He was backing her into a corner.

She couldn't—wouldn't—tell him she was leaving. Not like this. Stone would think she was leaving him because of his lack of faith—when restoring faith was her way back to heaven.

Back to Brooke.

"File for divorce?" His question stung deep in her heart. "Walk out that door?"

"I…" Dahlia's mind went blank and panic seized her. From somewhere in the house she heard a creaking sound and shuddered. "I don't know," she finally answered.

She watched him turn away and walk toward the windows. Wind and rain slashed at the house, causing creaking and groaning throughout.

Dahlia stood alone, hugging herself.

Chapter Nine

"But why can't we have pancakes again?" Shannon begged, climbing up on the stool. Dahlia placed a bowl of cold cereal in front of her, and the little girl asked, "What's this?"

"Just eat it," her father said, setting a glass of juice down for her.

"But—"

"Sweetie," Dahlia began, and Shannon looked up. "Sorry. Shannon, everyone's a little on edge this morning because of the storm."

"Is that like being nervous?"

Dahlia smiled at her. "That's it exactly."

"Okay." The little girl picked up her spoon and began eating.

Dahlia sipped her coffee and glanced uneasily out the window. The rain was coming down in sheets, the wind slamming into the house. And this was only the beginning. The lights had already flickered twice.

Setting her cup on the counter, Dahlia walked over to

the foot of the steps and called up to Field. There was no answer.

"Ah, to be able to sleep the sleep of the innocent," Rocky drawled, coming over to her.

And Blade put in, "It takes more than a hurricane to wake that boy."

"Yes, but—"

Stone smoothly interrupted. "We're all up earlier than usual. Let him sleep a little longer."

She glanced quickly at him. It was still early, not yet seven, but Dahlia couldn't shake the feeling that something was wrong.

"How can that child sleep through this?" she asked, making a gesture toward the window.

"I had to wake up Shannon," Flint offered with a teasing grin.

Dahlia sighed, aware that the whole family knew she was afraid of storms. The only reason the guys were up so early was because of the last-minute preparations they needed to make this morning, checking and rechecking the safety of the animals and the storage of extra supplies.

She'd been up strictly because of her phobia.

Dahlia's glance strayed once more toward Stone, who was checking out the first aid kit for the third time on the kitchen table. They'd silently declared a truce until the hurricane was over.

And then what?

The question popped into her mind, unwanted and intrusive. Dahlia wrapped her hands around the post and glanced once again upstairs. Shannon had only risen a short time ago. It wouldn't hurt to let Field sleep a little longer. He might even be getting dressed or brushing his teeth and hadn't heard her calling to him.

"Stone, you checked on him earlier, didn't you?" She turned anxiously to face him.

Stone nodded. "Twice. He'd thrown his covers off about two. And I checked on him again around five. He was all bundled up again and sound asleep, so I didn't go in."

"What were you checking for?" Shannon asked, turning around on the breakfast stool to face her uncle.

Stone smiled. "If he was warm enough. Or if he was asleep."

"Why?"

"Because that's what parents do when they love their kids," Flint answered his inquisitive six-year-old. "Here, eat some toast. I put jelly on it."

"Why?"

"Because strawberry jelly's your favorite."

"Oh, *Daddy!*" Shannon rolled her eyes. "I meant why do parents look to see if their kids are asleep? To chase out monsters?"

"Yes. To chase away the monsters."

"Like Woolly?"

Flint suppressed a smile. "Like Woolly."

"Who the heck is Woolly?" Rocky asked curiously, looking up from spreading cream cheese on a toasted bagel.

"Woolly is the monster who lives under my bed," Shannon told him primly.

Rocky looked bewildered, his gaze darting to Flint. "She has a monster named Woolly and a puppy named Fluffy?"

They laughed, prompting Blade to remind Rocky, "I seem to remember you had a monster living in your closet. What was his name?"

"Zeke," Stone supplied, grinning. "Named after the little bully in first grade."

"Hey, I'd forgotten that!"

"Guys! Do you mind?" Dahlia blurted out. She was in

no mood for this. "I—I'm sorry," she said when the four of them looked at her. "I'm going to check on Field," she added in a rush and hurried up the steps.

She knocked on Field's bedroom door, and when there was no answer, she quietly entered the room. "Hey, sleepy-head," she said softly. "Time to get up."

There was no answer from the sleeping lump under the covers.

"Field? Sweetie, time for breakfast." Dahlia crossed the room and touched the sleeping form. It felt...odd. "Field?" She shook the form as a slow, mounting horror started somewhere deep in her heart. *"Field?"*

Dahlia flung back the covers and found a sleeping bag and deflated basketball in the middle of the bed.

"Oh, no," she breathed. "Oh, no!"

She remained frozen for an instant, then went on a frantic search of his room. She was downstairs in the kitchen within minutes. "Stone! Stone, Field's gone," she announced as she rushed into the kitchen. "His jeans and boots and all-weather jacket are missing. So is his backpack and his gold nugget and the knife Rocky gave him."

Stone and his brothers stared back at her for what seemed like forever, shock and disbelief evident on their faces. Then Stone said tightly, "He couldn't be far. He was in bed at five—"

"No, he wasn't," Dahlia cut in. "That's what he wanted us to think, but he wasn't there. It was his sleeping bag and an old basketball under the covers."

Flint asked quickly, "What else is missing? How much money does he have with him?"

Rocky brushed past Dahlia and headed up the stairs to check.

"I'll see if he took any food with him." Flint hurried into the well-stocked pantry.

"He's not far," Blade assured them, putting a comforting hand on Stone's shoulder.

Dahlia merely stared back at her husband, feeling suddenly light-headed and dizzy. Oh, God, this couldn't be happening. Field was out there in this weather? With the hurricane headed straight toward them?

Stone appeared incapable of moving, but Blade hurried forward and slipped his arm around her. Dahlia leaned gratefully into him. Her eyes never left Stone's face.

"But why?" he said, almost to himself.

"Field said he'd run away," Shannon announced from the breakfast stool.

The three adults turned to her. Stone asked gently, "Honey, did he tell you that?"

Shannon nodded, her long dark braid bouncing down her back.

"When?"

The little girl scrunched up her face as she tried hard to remember.

"Yesterday. And before."

"He said it twice?" Dahlia asked.

Shannon nodded again. "He didn't want you to fight anymore. Said he'd run away."

Stone and Dahlia looked at each other, the same thoughts rushing through them. Had Field heard them last night? Was that why he'd run away?

Flint came back into the kitchen. "The pantry's been ransacked by little hands," he reported. "Cookies, breakfast bars, crackers and a jar of peanut butter."

"And his canteen's missing," Rocky said, coming down the steps. "So is the money he had stashed in his desk drawer."

"He had about fifty dollars he was saving for a new

bike,'' Stone added, grabbing his yellow rain slicker from the coat tree by the back door. ''Let's go.''

His three brothers moved toward the door, and Dahlia followed them. But as she was reaching for her raincoat, Stone said, ''You'd better stay here. In case he comes back,'' he added quickly, when Dahlia opened her mouth to tell him exactly what he could do with that suggestion.

''But…but where are you going to look for him?'' she asked, looking frantically out the window. ''The hurricane's almost on top of us.''

Stone snapped the last buttons on his slicker, then reached out to rub his knuckles gently over her right cheek. ''We'll find him.'' His voice was low, his gaze reaching into hers, begging her to trust him. ''We'll check the ranch first.''

Damn! Dahlia exploded inside when they went out into the wind and the rain. Field had several hours head start on them. And even if he hadn't left the ranch, it was not going to be easy to find him and bring him home before the hurricane hit. The Tyler Ranch was too big, too spread out, even with most of the ranch hands to help.

Where was he? Her heart cried out the question. And why had he left without talking to her about it?

Oh, but how could he? Dahlia railed in self-contempt. She'd been so busy trying to restore Stone's faith that she had done nothing to restore Field's faith in his own parents! She'd been so heaven-bent to get back to Brooke, she'd completely ignored Field's very real need for love and reassurance!

He must have felt so lost and alone to have taken off without a word to anyone.

''Aunt Dahlia?''

Dahlia whirled at the sound of Shannon's small, scared little voice. ''Oh…Shannon. What is it?''

"Will Field be okay?" Her gray-green eyes were wide and frightened.

"Oh, honey, of course he will." Dahlia hugged her close, ignoring the bits of jelly on the child's mouth.

He had to be, Dahlia thought painfully. If anything happened to Field…

Stone wouldn't be able to stand it, and neither would she. Dahlia silently prayed that their son would be safe and home before the hurricane came through. She gently wiped Shannon's face and hands with a damp paper towel, hugged her again and encouraged the little girl to go and get her crayons and new coloring book—all the time praying for Field's safety.

She had to keep busy. She had to do something. Dahlia started cleaning the kitchen, giving her hands something to do. But inside, her conflicting thoughts and feelings tumbled around, threatening to overwhelm her.

How had this happened? Why had it happened? Why was their son out there in the rain, when he should be safe in this house with the two of them? Because he no longer felt safe with his own parents? He no longer felt loved?

Oh, God, was that it? He no longer felt safe or secure with her, or with Stone?

Dahlia polished the counters with a dry dish towel, rubbing, rubbing away at the surface as though somehow she could rub out the past months.

Memories tore through her. Memories of this past year with its awful silence. And then the silence had been broken when the first anniversary of Brooke's death had unexpectedly crept closer, sending Stone and her into a tailspin of grief and anger and gut-wrenching guilt.

"Aunt Dahlia?"

Dahlia turned. Shannon stood in the doorway, clutching her coloring book and box of crayons to her chest. Forcing a smile, Dahlia held out her hand and drew the small child over to the table where they could color together.

For forty minutes they colored the pictures, side by side, in total silence. The wind whipped the rain against the windows in the breakfast nook. Dahlia looked up once to see Tony, one of their younger ranch hands, pause outside to check the windows. These windows were sheltered from the worst of the wind, unlike the ones in front that had already been boarded up.

She waved to him and he waved back.

"Aunt Dahlia, does this look like Field's cave?"

Dahlia glanced at the picture of Barbie at the entrance to a cave, under an outcropping of rocks Shannon had colored purple. "I guess so." She smiled and turned her attention back to watching Tony. But then the importance of Shannon's statements suddenly penetrated. "Field's cave?"

Shannon nodded without looking up, already absorbed in making Barbie's shirt cobalt blue.

Dahlia touched her hand. "Shannon, listen to me. It's important." When the little girl looked at her, she asked, "What did you mean by Field's cave?"

"He has a cave."

"A pretend cave."

Shannon shook her head. "A real one."

The Tyler Caves! "Shannon," Dahlia said carefully, "how do you know this?"

"Field told me."

"When?"

"Yesterday." Shannon suddenly looked scared. "He told me not to tell!" She popped both hands across her mouth, her eyes wide.

"Shannon, sweetie, think carefully. What else did Field say?" Dahlia's heart was pounding. But she had to ask the right questions if she wanted answers. "Why did Field want to keep the cave a secret?" She gently pulled the child's hands away from her mouth and held them.

"He was going to live there," Shannon said.

Dahlia was confused. "Live there?"

"If he had to go 'way to school."

"Field was going to go to the cave and live there if he was sent away to boarding school?" Dahlia's heart constricted painfully.

Shannon nodded.

"Shannon, where—" Dahlia broke off, because what was the use? Shannon would have no idea where the cave was. Dahlia knew there were caves on the ranch; Stone had taken her to them once, when they were first married. His father had named them the Tyler Caves when he was a child. And Stone and his brothers had spent many hours exploring them when they were boys.

But the caves had been boarded up for years.

Dahlia bit her lower lip as she considered the information she'd been given. Then she leaped up and ran to the back door, flinging it open and calling for Tony.

"Who else is here?"

"Just me." The young man stood inside the doorway, looking anxiously at her. "The rest are looking for Field. Do you need something?"

"Do you know where the Tyler Caves are?"

He shook his head. "I've been here four years. Haven't heard a word about any caves."

Dahlia sighed. She turned and grabbed her multicolored raincoat. "Tony, I want you to stay here with Shannon. Don't leave her alone for an instant. When the others come back, tell them I've gone to the caves. Tell them I believe that's where Field is."

"I can't let you do that. Stone would have my head on a—"

"I'll take full responsibility." Dahlia pushed past him. "You just take care of Shannon."

Dahlia closed the door behind her and headed for the stables. She had a vague idea where the caves were located, and she prayed she'd find her way to them.

She had no other choice. She had to find her son and get him to safety before the hurricane reached them.

Stone and Rocky wearily dismounted by the stables. They needed fresh horses, but Stone barely had the patience to saddle another one. They'd spent nearly half the morning searching for his son, but it was as though the child had vanished.

And the hurricane was starting to move through.

"Stone!" Tony came running toward them, visibly agitated and upset. He shouted over the fury of the wind and rain. "Dahlia took off for the Tyler Caves—"

"The caves!" Rocky whirled from securing the final strap on his horse. "Why didn't we think—"

"She went alone?"

Tony took a step backward in reaction to the fury in Stone's voice. "I couldn't go after her unless I left Shannon alone."

Panic surged through Stone like a tidal wave. Field and Dahlia were at the caves? The caves he and his brothers used to play in as children? The ones with all the deep, dark chambers? The ones that were dangerous, that had been carefully boarded up to prevent this from ever happening? How was this possible?

"Field must have found one of the caves," Rocky suggested. "A likely place to hide, too. And good protection from the hurricane."

"If he didn't break his neck falling off one of the ledges." Stone swung a leg up over his horse and rode off.

Why in hell had she gone off like that? The question curled up inside of Stone and dug in hard. Dahlia didn't know where the caves were. Not really. She only knew the general location. Why hadn't she waited? Why was she risking her life this way? She could easily get lost in the hills, especially in the wind and the rain—

Stone reined in his panic. He had to stay calm. He had to. If he didn't, he'd never find Dahlia and Field.

"Field's probably in that first cave!" Rocky shouted to him from behind. "The one with the two boulders shoved into the entrance!"

Stone nodded. That had been his first thought, too. There was enough room for a child to slip between the rocks and get inside. And enough room for a small, slender woman like Dahlia to also get through—if she hadn't gotten herself lost along the way.

Dahlia was lost.

It had taken her forever to find the Tyler Caves—but now what? Which one was Field hiding in?

"Field!" she shouted in growing terror. "Field!"

Where was he? Which cave had he gone into? She'd stumbled across two of them. One was boarded up and the other one had huge rocks wedged in the entrance. Dahlia didn't see how Field could possibly have managed to get into either one.

How many caves were there? Two? Seven? A dozen? She couldn't remember.

Oh please, please help me find the right one! Dahlia's breathing was shallow and ragged as she moved her flashlight in a wide arc, searching for more of the caves. But the rain made visibility difficult and the wind made it next to impossible for her to hear anything.

Behind her a tree limb crashed to the ground, narrowly missing her, and Dahlia flung herself against the boulders at the entrance to one of the caves. The outcropping of rocks provided a small degree of shelter from the rain. She stood there, watching the trees bend almost to the ground, the rain coming down in sheets.

Her little boy was out in this!

"Field!" Dahlia screamed as panic ripped through her. "Field! Where are you?"

She was there when he'd taken his first steps, and when he'd entered first grade. She'd held his hand the first time Field had attempted to climb the porch steps, and let go of his hand when he was ready to climb them alone.

She wanted to be there for him always and forever— when he graduated from high school, when he brought home the woman he wanted to marry, when he had his first child....

"Field!" Dahlia screamed, knowing he couldn't hear her. Maybe he'd never hear her again.

She huddled near the rocks, wondering what to do. Her horse was near, but should she ride farther into the hills, searching out each cave until she found him? Or should she turn back and get help?

No! She had no time to get help! She had to do this alone. And she would do it. She'd find Field herself.

Taking a deep, steadying breath, she turned on her flashlight again and slowly scanned the area, trying to see if she'd overlooked anything. What had Stone and his brothers said about the caves?

There were several of them, but how many?

Four! There were four of them! Dahlia felt elated. One cave named for each brother. That was it. Okay. She took another deep, calming breath and swallowed. She'd found two of them; she could find the others.

She was just about to step away from the cave when she noticed what she'd been too scared and distracted to notice before. There was a space between the boulders.

A space large enough for a child or a small adult.

Dahlia gripped her heavy-duty flashlight and slipped between the rocks and entered the cave. These caves had chambers, she remembered. This one seemed large and roomy, she noticed in relief, scanning the chamber with her flashlight. And awfully quiet.

"Field?" Dahlia called out. "Field, are you in here? It's Mom!"

Nothing.

"Field?" She said it loudly and waited.

Then she heard a small, muffled voice coming from the far side of the chamber. "Mom? Is that you?"

Oh, God, thank you! Dahlia's sob of relief caught in her throat. She moved forward in a rush, wanting to haul him close and hold him and keep him safe.

Dahlia reached the entrance to a second chamber just as Field called out, "Mom, be careful of—"

Too late.

She stepped off a ledge and felt herself falling down, down, down....

She was drifting up, up, up....

Drifting through the warm mist.

"Mom? Mom, please wake up."

Field's voice.

"Mom!"

Dahlia struggled to answer him. He sounded scared, and she needed to reassure him. But she kept drifting upward, floating on air. And she felt warm and sleepy.

"I'm sorry, Mom. I'm sorry."

No, Field, don't be sorry. This wasn't your fault. Too much guilt. Too much...

A small hand touched her face. A gentle caress, light as a feather, but warm and solid. "Mom, you're bleeding."

I'm okay, Field. I'm okay. Don't be scared. It's so comfortable here. And I feel so safe.

"I have to get help." His voice was shaking with emotion, but there was a decisive edge to it that penetrated the soft, warm mist she was floating in. "I have to leave you and get help," he repeated.

The mist swirled and shifted uncomfortably beneath her. Dahlia was filled with sudden panic. *No!* she screamed from somewhere deep inside. *No, Field, don't go out there! Stay here! Stay inside the cave!*

Dahlia felt something firm and solid shoved into her hand. "Here's your flashlight." Her fingers automatically closed around it. "Hold on, Mom. I'll be back."

I'll be back.

Those had been Brooke's words when she'd left the house that morning a year ago. I'll be back, Mom, to clean my room.

And Dahlia never saw her alive again.

I'll be back, Mom.

Hold on, Mom. I'll be back.

I'll be back.

The words and voices and faces of her two children blended into one, then separated once more.

Field. He couldn't go outside the cave. The hurricane was almost on top of them! He'd be killed!

Oh, no! No! Field had to be kept safe! No matter what, he had to grow up strong and whole!

Dahlia fought the warm mist as it carried her upward, away from Field and Stone.

No!

Dahlia struggled against the chilling, clinging dampness. She fought hard to open her eyes and reach for her son's hand.

She had to reassure him. She couldn't let him go outside. She just couldn't. He'd get lost out there. The stream was rising higher with each passing second.

He'd have to cross the stream in order to get help, in order to get back to the ranch. She'd had a hard time getting across it herself.

Field would drown in the swollen stream!

Dahlia opened her mouth to scream out the injustice of this—but she couldn't make a sound.

She was caught up in the mist and drifting far above the cave.

Drifting up, up, up…

She drifted up, up, up into the mist.

And suddenly found herself standing alone by a gate. Dahlia gripped the flashlight Field had given her, and ran her thumb gently over the thick, rubber handle as she looked around in confusion.

A white picket fence enclosed a pretty yard, with flowers of every color blooming in wide borders along the fence. The mist blurred the edges of the picture-perfect setting, but inside the yard Dahlia could see the blue sky and sunshine, and smell the flowers. She also spotted an enormous, lovely maple tree—

And Brooke!

A cry of joy escaped her.

Her daughter was sitting on a bench beneath the ancient shade tree, carefully making a wreath of flowers from the supply in the garden. She wore jeans and a short-sleeved denim shirt, embroidered with pink flowers on the collar, her dark hair flowing down her back. Dahlia watched as her daughter finished the wreath of pink and white flowers, and placed it on the back of her head.

Brooke looked up and ran toward her. They met at the gate and touched hands, fingers entwining.

"Mom, what are you doing here?"

Brooke appeared genuinely surprised to see her, Dahlia thought in considerable confusion. "Do I need my ticket to come through the gate?" she asked her.

"Ticket?" Brooke looked confused.

Dahlia looked around for Basil as she searched the pockets of her jeans and raincoat. Where on earth was the ticket he had given her? Come to think of it, she hadn't seen that ticket since she'd left Basil and tumbled back to earth. Was that why she hadn't been able to get back here? Dahlia wondered. Because she'd lost her ticket?

"Mom. Mom," Brooke said softly, capturing her free hand in hers again. "You're not supposed to be here."

Dahlia noticed the stack of books by the bench. And the sketchbook and easel, and collection of art supplies.

A beautiful and warm place to spend eternity in.

"I...I came back to be with you," Dahlia said slowly, feasting her eyes on her little girl. Oh, she wanted so much to hold her tightly, to sit with her in this beautiful place. "Didn't Basil tell you I was returning?"

"Basil? Who's that?"

"Well, Basil is—" Dahlia stopped in mid-sentence, because Brooke was frowning up at her, blue eyes puzzled. "Honey, don't you know who Basil is?"

Brooke shook her head.

Something was wrong. If Basil was indeed the chief angel, then wouldn't Brooke know it? Isn't that how it worked?

"Brooke, I was here...before. More than two weeks ago," she stammered, gripping her daughter's small hands.

"Mom, you were never here. I would have known," Brooke added gently when Dahlia opened her mouth to protest.

She was never here? She'd never been to the gates of heaven?

She'd never been an angel?

Everything she'd believed in the past two weeks was unraveling all around her.

"But I was here! I know I was!" Dahlia burst out in frustration. "Basil gave me a ticket, and I was all ready to go through the gate and get my wings and halo, but Basil stopped me."

Brooke remained silent.

"Basil said I had three weeks to restore your dad's faith. If I did that, then I could return to heaven and be with you," Dahlia explained.

Brooke searched Dahlia's face for an instant, and then she said gently, "You were never here, Mom. Sometimes in our grief we're willing to believe anything to make the pain go away and to hold on to the people we love."

Was...was Brooke saying that Stone had been right all along?

She'd never been an angel?

It had all been in her mind from the very beginning?

She looked into the eyes of the child standing before her. The little girl who would never grow to adulthood. Her seven-year-old daughter who had the wisdom of the ages in her clear blue gaze.

"I wanted to be with you so badly," Dahlia admitted in a small voice. "I've felt so lost and alone without you. I would have done anything to be with you again. Even believe I was an angel, I guess."

"It's time to let go, Mom."

Time to let go. That was what Stone had told her earlier.

Time to let go. To say goodbye to her baby girl. To fight for her life. To fight for her family.

A wave of pure understanding smashed through Dahlia, leaving a single, perfect shell gleaming on the wet sand of her consciousness. She'd been the one unable to deal with Brooke's death. She'd been so wrapped up in her own pain she'd been totally oblivious to Stone's for an entire year.

Believing she was an angel had been her subconscious attempt to reunite her family. But she'd selfishly thought that if she convinced Stone to keep Field with him on the ranch, then she could be with Brooke in heaven.

What price had she paid for her selfishness?

The price was Stone's happiness and Field's. And her own. She'd sacrificed the present and the future to live in the past with a child who would never be as she once was— a little girl who needed her mommy. Brooke was an angel now, a beautiful angel, and her home was in heaven.

And Dahlia's home was on earth.

She knew there was much joy and happiness waiting for her—if she only had the faith and the love and the trust to reach for it. And to hold on to it.

Brooke smiled happily at her. "I love you, Mom."

"I love you." Dahlia barely got the words out before Brooke stepped back, away from her.

The mist suddenly appeared, then swirled and shifted beneath her feet.

Dahlia was tumbling down, down, down…

Chapter Ten

Stone couldn't believe this was happening. Not again. And not to both Dahlia and Field. The two of them were lost to him just as surely as Brooke. The wind and rain slashed at him as he rode toward the caves. He rode too close to a tree, and a slender branch hit him in the face, but he didn't notice. He kept going.

He had to keep going. He forced himself to ride onward, to move forward—and not to look back.

Because what good did it do to look back, anyway? That was all he'd been doing for a solid year. Looking back and wishing for things that could never be again.

Like having Brooke back with them.

But she wasn't coming back. And he'd risked the love and happiness of those closest to him, instead of facing the fact of her death months ago. No matter how much guilt he took upon his own shoulders, his little girl was dead, and nothing, absolutely nothing, was going to bring her back to him.

Dahlia and Field meant everything to him. They were

his whole life. He should have been looking ahead and taking care of the family he had left.

Why hadn't he done that?

The question roared through him with all the fierceness of the wind hammering at the space around him.

The answer made no difference in the long run. The fact was, he hadn't tried to build a new life without Brooke in it. Guilt had blocked everything out. Blocked out all the air and life and energy and love.

For his son—and his wife.

Field had run away from home during a hurricane, just to get some semblance of peace and quiet in his life.

Dahlia had run off to try and join the angels in heaven to get the love and security she'd needed from him.

And here he was chasing after both of them, being chased by a hurricane—and they were all running out of time.

"Stone!" Rocky suddenly reined in, and pointed at a horse in a meadow beside the trail.

Stone reined in beside him, twisting in his saddle to get a better view. Gray Cloud! What in hell was Field's horse doing this far away from the caves?

For an instant, Stone's mind went blank. But when the panic came, it was solid and dark and real. Had Gray Cloud thrown Field? Was his little boy lying dead in a ditch somewhere?

Rocky advanced upon the mare slowly by foot, and Stone held the reins of their two horses. Field had raised Gray Cloud from a foal, and that fact alone had caused Stone's panic attack to shift into high gear. Quarter horses were kind, gentle and loyal to their masters. They were also swift and surefooted on steep trails and across rushing water.

And nothing short of a full-scale hurricane could have caused the mare to have left Field behind.

Stone saw his brother grab hold of the mare's reins to lead her out of the meadow. The mare looked lost and frightened, but a quick visual examination showed no signs of injury.

Stone hoped like hell that was true for Field, too.

As if reading his thoughts, Rocky said, "Field's probably safe in the cave—"

"And he let Gray Cloud wander off alone?" Stone ran his gloved hand gently over the horse's mane.

"He's too smart a kid to have tied Gray Cloud up outside—not with the hurricane and all," Rocky shouted back over the noise of the wind.

A snap and crash behind them made them both whirl. A large oak tree had split down the middle and came crashing to the ground not ten feet behind them. The three horses started backing away, and it was all they could do to calm the trio.

"Take Gray Cloud and get back to the ranch!" Stone yelled to his brother.

"In your dreams!" Rocky yelled back.

"Rocky—"

"You coming or not?" Rain sheeted down Rocky's yellow rain slicker, and the wind splattered it in his face. But the green eyes hardened in grim determination.

Stone had seen the beginnings of that same expression in Field's eyes a few times recently. And he could only pray that he'd get the chance to see that look in his son's eyes as a teenager and as a young man.

Stone didn't want to risk his brother's life, but he also knew it was no use arguing with him, either. Rocky was sticking to him like glue today, and would continue to do so until Dahlia and Field were both found.

They heard the sounds of a horse and someone yelling over the roar of the wind and the rain. Stone turned and was stunned by what he saw. It was Dahlia's horse, but the small rider, holding on for dear life and riding hard toward them, was Field.

His son came off the horse almost before he'd reined in—and hurled himself into Stone's waiting arms. He was babbling incoherently, tears and rain running down his face, his gray eyes huge and terrified.

"Mom's hurt." Field's hands clutched Stone. "She's hurt bad. She's in the cave—the one with the rocks shoved into the entrance. She…she fell." Fresh tears spilled out as Field choked on a sob. "I couldn't get her to wake up."

Stone heard the words, but they made no sense to him. As fast as heart-stopping relief had poured in when he'd spotted Field riding toward him, it had rushed out again when he realized Dahlia was seriously hurt—and alone in the dark cave.

"I didn't want to leave her alone, but—"

"You did the right thing, Field," Stone hastened to say. He hugged his son and then released him. "It was a mature thing to come and get help, to do what needed to be done."

"But it's all my fault." The low voice was filled with angry self-contempt, the gaze steady and direct on Stone's face.

"It's no one's fault," Stone said gently. And he meant it to the depths of his soul.

"It's my fault. I ran away—"

"Field, listen to me." Stone cupped the child's head in both hands, forcing him to focus on what he was saying because he had only a moment to spare. "Sometimes things just happen. But no one's to blame. You weren't the cause of your mom getting hurt any more than I was the cause of Brooke getting killed. What happened to your mom was an accident. That's all it was. Okay?''

''Okay,'' came the quiet reply.

Stone turned his son over to Rocky with instructions to get Field back to the ranch, then he mounted up. The sky was dark, the clouds swirling into dangerous-looking spirals.

He rode off, hell-bent to get to the cave ahead of the hurricane.

Stone reined in hard at the swollen stream. How the hell had Field managed to cross this? Was it easier upstream? No, damn it, that was the long way around!

Stone urged his quarter horse closer to the water, but the animal whinnied and kept backing up. No matter what Stone did, the horse refused to cross the stream. The wind was cracking trees to the ground right and left of them. The noise level alone was enough to make the most obedient animal nervous and resistant to orders.

But Stone had to get them both across the stream and he had to do it now.

He dismounted and led the horse into the water, talking to him in low, gentle, soothing tones. The water wasn't all that deep, but it bubbled and churned over the rocks as the hurricane came through with a vengeance.

Halfway across, the horse finally noticed the opposite bank and happily pushed ahead. Stone hung on to him, and once free of the stream, mounted up and headed for the cave.

Only he couldn't find it.

He couldn't find the Tyler Caves.

Had he crossed the stream too soon? Or too late? Swearing steadily, he looked around to try and get his bearings—

but it was no use. The wind and the rain and the dark fury of the storm made everything look different.

Confusing.

Surreal.

He'd grown up here! He sure as hell should be able to find the damn caves!

They were arranged in a wide, lopsided triangle, with the one Field had chosen as a hideout at the tip. Another cave was at the right, and two more stretched out toward the left.

But he saw nothing that looked the way it should.

The horse beneath him started to sidestep and whinny, rolling his head with increasing agitation. Stone glanced back over his shoulder and stared up at the sky in blank horror.

A twister!

It wasn't unusual for hurricanes to spawn tornadoes, but it was unusual for Stone to be out in the open when it hit!

Going on blind faith in his own instincts, Stone kicked his horse into a gallop, believing the caves were farther upstream. There was simply no way to tell where the twister would land, what path it would take or if it would suddenly take itself elsewhere. But Stone wasn't going to stick around long enough to find out.

He rode hard toward what must be the Tyler Caves, but once more he found himself turned around and floundering for direction. He reined in and looked around once more. The hurricane hammered away at the ranch, the trees snapping to the ground with a heartbreaking crunch—and he was lost. *Infuriatingly lost!*

But then he saw something ahead of him. A flash of white mist, briefly taking the shape of a small child. She wore wings, halo, a long white dress—and a wreath of pink and white flowers in her hair.

She looked up at him.

Brooke?

She beckoned him to follow her, and Stone did. Then he saw it. The two familiar-looking boulders shoved into the entrance of the cave. He dismounted. He'd have to move one of them to get inside, but he had all the faith he needed to get the job done.

He'd been running on faith all morning. Faith that they'd somehow get through this.

But more importantly—faith in himself.

Stone looked back to where he'd last seen the small wispy angel with his daughter's face—but the apparition had disappeared.

But he'd be forever grateful to whoever—or whatever—had led him to Dahlia.

She was tumbling down, down, down....

Dahlia was conscious of something solid taking shape in the swirling white mist. She opened her eyes and looked up at Stone.

And smiled with true joy and happiness in her heart. And love.

Dahlia struggled to sit up, but Stone held her still. "Don't move," he said gently, stroking her hair back from her face.

She didn't protest. She stared into his beautiful gray eyes, shadowed with fatigue. "Your face is all scratched," she said.

"A branch hit me."

Light filtered in from the outer cave chamber, enough for her to see her husband and her immediate surroundings. Her head was cushioned on what smelled like a vinyl rain slicker.

"You moved the rocks to get in?" Dahlia asked.

"One of them." Stone was busy taking her pulse and she watched him.

And listened to the muted fury of the hurricane outside the cave.

"You can let go of the flashlight now," Stone said gently. "You've had a death grip on it since I've been here."

"I was holding on to life," she answered.

Stone grew still. "It's about time," he said softly, flashing her a grin.

Dahlia smiled back, and stayed very quiet while his hands roamed over her, checking for broken bones and cuts and bruises. She was still in a semidrowsy state, but it was a pleasant feeling.

Until she remembered what she was doing here.

"Field!" Dahlia sat up, grabbing for Stone's arm. "Is he—"

"He's fine." Stone leaned over her, wrapping his rain slicker around her for warmth. "He's back at the ranch safe and sound. You scared him to death."

"I know." Dahlia's voice was contrite.

"What was the big idea coming out here alone?" he asked. He produced a small first aid kit that he always kept in his saddlebags, and dabbed disinfectant on a small cut on her ankle.

Dahlia noticed that her right forearm had already been bandaged with gauze and tape. It was stiff and sore and beginning to hurt. "How long have you been here?"

"Long enough to keep you from bleeding to death. Why didn't you wait for me?"

"I couldn't," she said simply, truthfully. "What happened to my arm?"

"You have a narrow, deep cut from the top of your wrist

to your elbow." Stone touched her face with his fingers and she didn't think he was checking for injuries now.

She smiled happily at him and watched the gray of his eyes deepen into pewter.

"I'm incredibly thirsty," she said suddenly.

He tossed the tube of disinfectant into the first aid kit and handed her a canteen of water. "Drink it slowly," he cautioned.

Dahlia nodded and sipped the cool water. "I thought I had hit my head again."

"You were lucky you weren't killed. What did you do— run in here without looking first?"

Dahlia smiled at the soft irritation in his voice. It didn't match the deep concern she saw in his eyes. She gripped the canteen with one hand and took another thirsty sip. Lowering it to her lap, she looked at him. "I have a lot to tell you."

"Nothing matters now—just as long as you're okay." Stone tucked a lock of hair behind her ear, his fingers lingering longer than necessary.

"I'm fine. Really," she said quietly, looking into his worried gray eyes. "A little weak, a little sore, but…I think the fall off that ledge knocked some sense into me."

That got his full attention.

"I never was an angel," she told him slowly as she reached out with her good hand, entwining her fingers through his. "But I didn't lie to you—"

"Don't you think I know that?" The words sounded wrenched out of him, as though from somewhere deep within. Perhaps from the bottom of his heart.

"I'm so sorry for what I put you through these past few weeks," Dahlia rushed on, needing to get everything out in the open between them. "I think my head injury and slipping into a coma so close to the first anniversary of Brooke's death just…put me over the top emotionally.''

"It's okay, you don't have to explain.''

But Dahlia needed to explain. She needed to make him understand why she'd put him through hell by believing she was an angel. "I think, maybe, that's where I got the idea I only had three weeks to convince you. Because the three weeks are up…the first anniversary of Brooke's death.''

He nodded, acceptance in his clear gray gaze.

"Stone, I'm sorry,'' she said again.

But he was shaking his head. Their fingers tightened around each other's and the healing began. Dahlia knew it would be a hard road to travel, but their love would help them to deal with Brooke's death.

After the longest time, when the gentle, peaceful silence continued to ebb and flow around them, Stone asked, "What made you change your mind? About being an angel.''

Dahlia sighed. "I don't know where to start. It's so…complicated.''

He grinned easily. "Start at the beginning.'' He settled down next to her, gathering her into a gentle embrace. "Looks like we're going to be here awhile.''

They were both silent for an instant, as they listened to the fury of the hurricane, just a short distance away. But Dahlia felt safe and sheltered in the depths of the cave, and in the arms of her husband.

"It's kind of cozy in here, isn't it?'' she said with a smile, her gaze locking on his.

"Very cozy. Warm, fuzzy feelings and everything.''

Dahlia smiled. "I'm almost afraid to tell you what happened,'' she admitted. What if he didn't believe her?

The brief, teasing look in Stone's eyes muted into gentle understanding. "Tell me anyway."

Dahlia took a deep breath and plunged forward. "I had another dream—when I fell." She kept her eyes focused on the opposite wall of the cave. "I saw…Brooke. And she said I'd never been to the gates of heaven, that she would have known if I'd been there." Dahlia stole a look at him and was relieved to see Stone truly listening to her. "Brooke told me that sometimes we're willing to do anything to make the pain of grief go away."

Dahlia stopped talking for a moment to nestle closer. "I wanted so much to reunite our family, to make us whole again—"

"But you couldn't do it alone," Stone broke in to say. "I was fighting you every step of the way."

"You were right to fight me." Dahlia took a deep breath and let it out briskly. "I demanded that life should get back to normal only a few weeks after Brooke died. I made the decision to have another baby nine months ago, Stone, without even bothering to ask how you felt about it. Without giving you the time you needed to grieve…"

Stone pulled her a little closer and brushed a kiss against her cheek. "You were reaching out for something you'd lost," he told her softly. "The best way you knew how."

"It was the way I was raised—to move forward, to push on, no matter what the circumstances. No matter how much I might need to grieve myself," she said thoughtfully. "Moving around the way I did, leaving friends and family behind, I was never allowed to show any fear or sense of loss."

Dahlia had talked to Stone about her life growing up, but she'd perfected the art of blocking out the painful memories of moving around so much, the loneliness and isolation, the total disruption of her life year after year after year.

"Each time we moved," she told him now, "I'd lose more friends. I wasn't allowed to talk about the house we left or our friends and neighbors. The way I learned to cope as a small child was to pretend."

"What did you pretend?"

Dahlia heard the gentle amusement in his voice and smiled faintly as she remembered. "I'd pretend our new house was where I was born. That I had grandparents and aunts and uncles and cousins who lived around the corner. And that every child I'd ever met lived on the same street as I did."

"And when you were older?"

Dahlia shrugged. "I pretended it didn't matter. I pretended living in a new place was an exciting new adventure. Out with the old, in with the new—that was my motto for survival," she added painfully.

"And then Brooke died." His hand had a death grip on hers. "And I shut you out."

He did understand!

Then she said, "The worst part was when you wouldn't let me talk about Brooke, the same way I had been expected, as a child growing up, to keep my mouth shut and suffer in silence. But Brooke was my daughter, my own child. Losing her wasn't like losing a friend because I'd moved to another part of the world. I needed to talk about her, to validate her life by keeping all the memories of her alive. Not talking about her felt like…like you wanted to erase her from our hearts," she accused honestly.

"I'm sorry." Stone took a deep, ragged breath. Staring up at the ceiling of the cave, he said tightly, "But talking about her, remembering her, was so hard. All I could remember was giving her that horse—"

"Stone, it wasn't your fault Brooke died." Dahlia sat up, pushing his hands away when he tried to make her sit still. She turned to face him. "Brooke disobeyed the first rule we taught her—never get near one of the animals without an adult present. What happened to her was no one's fault. It was an accident."

Stone's gaze was gentle on her face. "That's almost exactly what I told Field today. He blamed himself for your getting hurt—"

"Oh, no!" Dahlia was horrified. "Oh, Stone..."

"He's been through a hell of a lot this past year." Stone picked up the canteen she'd momentarily set aside. "Drink some more water. And try to sit quietly. I'm not going to talk to you if you don't stop bouncing around like a jumping bean."

Dahlia did as she was told, sipping water carefully as she listened to Stone's next words.

"I think I wanted to feel the pain of losing Brooke," he said, his voice low. "I think that's why I kept shutting down whenever you tried to talk to me and share our memories of her. I didn't want to remember the good times, because it hurt too much. It was much easier just to feel the pain—as a kind of penance for allowing her to die."

"But you didn't *let* her die. Damn it, you gave her a beautiful, gentle horse of her own. Exactly what she'd wanted—a golden palomino named Firelight."

Dahlia studied him a moment, thinking hard. "I know I thought Brooke was too young for a horse of her own," she told him gently. "But what do I know about horses and little kids? Field had his own horse—"

"But Field raised Gray Cloud from a foal."

"You mean, you and Field did. And when he was trained, Gray Cloud was given to Field on his seventh birthday," Dahlia shot back. "The same way you and Brooke raised Firelight as a special birthday gift for her seventh birthday. And you set down clear-cut rules for both of them. Only one morning Brooke, on impulse, chose not to obey them,'' she said painfully. ''Or she forgot them. But what happened was not your fault.''

Stone's sigh seemed to come from deep inside his soul. ''I know all that.''

''Do you? Stone, she would have been heartbroken if we'd made her wait another year. Getting a horse at seven is a Tyler family ritual, and a nice one.'' Dahlia leaned in, trying to get a closer look at his face. ''You still believe that, don't you? That it's nice for a Tyler child to look forward to certain events that mark his path to adulthood?''

''Yeah.'' Stone looked at her, gratitude in his eyes. ''I still believe in family traditions.''

''I thought you'd lost your faith,'' she said. ''Turned out, I lost mine somewhere along the way, too. All we can do is love each other and Field, and do the best we can. But we have to believe in ourselves, Stone, and our life together. We need to trust ourselves and each other—that's the true angel, you know. Faith.''

''How did you get so wise?''

''I've been hanging out with angels lately,'' she returned with a grin. ''Even if they were only in my mind. Or sort of in my mind,'' she added ruefully.

Something flickered across Stone's face. Something… odd.

He cleared his throat. ''I saw something out there when I was searching for this cave. It was dark and the wind was blowing hard, the rain was coming down in buckets—and I may have imagined it. I don't know.'' He paused for a heartbeat. ''But I saw her…or something—''

''Her?''

"Brooke," Stone said softly. "I saw Brooke. She led me to you."

"Did she have a wreath of flowers in her hair?" Dahlia asked him quickly.

Stone nodded. Their gazes met and held endlessly. Then he said, "Pink and white ones."

Dahlia was struck by a sudden wondrous joy. "Stone, do you think…? Is it possible—"

"I don't know. But something led me to you." He pulled her to him and held her close. "I was all turned around. I couldn't find the caves. And if I hadn't found you, if I'd waited until the hurricane had passed through—"

Dahlia snuggled deeper into his arms. "We've been given a second chance, you know."

Stone's mouth hovered a mere inch above hers. "Which we're going to make the most of. Just as soon as you recover from this latest fall." He grinned, and then kissed her warmly, gently. A kiss with great promise.

"I love you," he told her softly.

Dahlia's happiness was complete. "I love you, too. Very much."

Being with Stone, holding him, touching him, was all Dahlia wanted or needed. All she'd ever needed. And as Stone cradled her against him to wait out the hurricane, Dahlia realized she'd always had her own personal, private heaven on earth.

Here on Tyler soil with this particular Tyler man.

* * * * *

This March Silhouette is proud to present

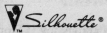

SENSATIONAL

MAGGIE SHAYNE
BARBARA BOSWELL
SUSAN MALLERY
MARIE FERRARELLA

This is a special collection of four complete novels for one low price, featuring a novel from each line: Silhouette Intimate Moments, Silhouette Desire, Silhouette Special Edition and Silhouette Romance.

Available at your favorite retail outlet.

If you enjoyed what you just read,
then we've got an offer you can't resist!

Take 2 bestselling
love stories FREE!
Plus get a FREE surprise gift!

Clip this page and mail it to Silhouette Reader Service™

IN U.S.A.
3010 Walden Ave.
P.O. Box 1867
Buffalo, N.Y. 14240-1867

IN CANADA
P.O. Box 609
Fort Erie, Ontario
L2A 5X3

YES! Please send me 2 free Silhouette Romance® novels and my free surprise gift. Then send me 6 brand-new novels every month, which I will receive months before they're available in stores. In the U.S.A., bill me at the bargain price of $2.90 plus 25¢ delivery per book and applicable sales tax, if any*. In Canada, bill me at the bargain price of $3.25 plus 25¢ delivery per book and applicable taxes**. That's the complete price and a savings of over 10% off the cover prices—what a great deal! I understand that accepting the 2 free books and gift places me under no obligation ever to buy any books. I can always return a shipment and cancel at any time. Even if I never buy another book from Silhouette, the 2 free books and gift are mine to keep forever. So why not take us up on our invitation. You'll be glad you did!

215 SEN CNE7
315 SEN CNE9

Name	(PLEASE PRINT)
Address	Apt.#
City	State/Prov.	Zip/Postal Code

* Terms and prices subject to change without notice. Sales tax applicable in N.Y.
** Canadian residents will be charged applicable provincial taxes and GST.
   All orders subject to approval. Offer limited to one per household.
   ® are registered trademarks of Harlequin Enterprises Limited.

SROM99   ©1998 Harlequin Enterprises Limited

SOMETIMES THE SMALLEST PACKAGES CAN LEAD TO THE BIGGEST SURPRISES!

February 1999
A VOW, A RING, A BABY SWING
by Teresa Southwick (SR #1349)

Pregnant and alone, Rosie Marchetti had just been stood up at the altar. So family friend Steve Schafer stepped up the aisle and married her. Now Rosie is trying to convince him that this family was meant to be....

May 1999
THE BABY ARRANGEMENT
by Moyra Tarling (SR #1368)

Jared McAndrew has been searching for his son, and when he discovers Faith Nelson with his child he demands she come home with him. Can Faith convince Jared that he has the wrong mother — but the right bride?

Enjoy these stories of love and family. And look for future BUNDLES OF JOY titles from Leanna Wilson and Suzanne McMinn coming in the fall of 1999.

BUNDLES OF JOY
only from

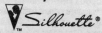

Available wherever Silhouette books are sold.

Look us up on-line at: http://www.romance.net

SRBOJJ-J

THESE BACHELOR DADS NEED A LITTLE TENDERNESS—AND A WHOLE LOT OF LOVING!

January 1999—A Rugged Ranchin' Dad
by Kia Cochrane (SR# 1343)

Tragedy had wedged Stone Tyler's family apart. Now this rugged rancher would do everything in his power to be the perfect daddy—and recapture his wife's heart—before time ran out....

April 1999 —Prince Charming's Return
by Myrna Mackenzie (SR# 1361)

Gray Alexander was back in town—and had just met the son he had never known he had. Now he wanted to make Cassie Pratt pay for her deception eleven years ago...even if the price was marriage!

And in **June 1999** don't miss Donna Clayton's touching story of Dylan Minster, a man who has been raising his daughter all alone....

Fall in love with our FABULOUS FATHERS!

And look for more FABULOUS FATHERS in the months to come. Only from

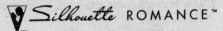

Available wherever Silhouette books are sold.

Look us up on-line at: http://www.romance.net   SRFFJ-J

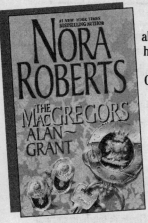

COMING NEXT MONTH

#1348 THE NIGHT BEFORE BABY—Karen Rose Smith
Loving the Boss

The rumors were true! Single gal Olivia McGovern was pregnant, and dashing Lucas Hunter was the father-to-be. So the honorable lawyer offered to marry Olivia for the baby's sake. But time spent in Olivia's loving arms had her boss looking for more than just "honor" from his wedded wife!

#1349 A VOW, A RING, A BABY SWING—Teresa Southwick
Bundles of Joy

Pregnant and alone, Rosie Marchetti had just been stood up at the altar. So family friend Steve Schafer stepped up the aisle and married her. And although Steve thought he wasn't good enough for the shy beauty, she was out to convince him that this family was meant to be....

#1350 BABY IN HER ARMS—Judy Christenberry
Lucky Charm Sisters

Josh McKinney had found his infant girl. Now he had to find a baby expert—quick! So he convinced charming Maggie O'Connor to take care of little Ginny. But the more time Josh spent with his temporary family, the more he wanted to make Maggie his real wife....

#1351 NEVER TOO LATE FOR LOVE—Marie Ferrarella
Like Mother, Like Daughter

CEO Bruce Reed thought his life was full—until he met the flirtatious Margo McCloud at his son's wedding. Her sultry voice permeated his dreams, and he wondered if his son had the right idea about marriage. But could he convince Margo that it wasn't too late for their love?

#1352 MR. RIGHT NEXT DOOR—Arlene James
He's My Hero

Morgan Holt was everything Denise Jenkins thought a hero should be—smart, sexy, intelligent—and he had swooped to her rescue by pretending to be her beloved. But if Morgan was busy saving Denise, who was going to save Morgan's heart from *her* once their romance turned real?

#1353 A FAMILY FOR THE SHERIFF—Elyssa Henry
Family Matters

Fall for a sheriff? Never! Maria Lightner had been hurt by doing that once before. But when lawman Joe Roberts strolled into her life, Maria took another look. And even though her head said he was wrong, her heart was telling her something altogether different....